From

the

Diaphragm

Saxon Bryce

From the Diaphragm

Saxon Bryce

Dedication

I dedicate this to all the storytellers who came before me. Without your melodious tales, I would not have been so motivated to create my stories inspired by your amazing works. I thank you.

Disclaimer

The titles come from the original works, but the tales I include are all from my own imagination; based, but not entirely, on the original songs. I would like to think you would take a little time to search for the songs I have chosen for From the Diaphragm, and listen to the melodies, the emotions, and the original thoughts behind each one.

Table of Contents

The Gypsy Rover

He loved whistling. Even more than that, he loved roaming the countryside, carefree and without a worry. His clothes, not of the best quality, his face and hands covered in sweat and dust from the road.

The wandering gypsy, hair tied back, pack slung over a shoulder, tired of whistling. His dry lips and parched throat complained. He tilted his head and listened for the sound of a stream or brook to whet his mouth.

He happened by Joy bathing her feet in a stream near her father's keep; holdings vast, pockets full. The successful Baron kept his daughter near. He had grand plans for her.

Gerhart, the gypsy, smiled. He heard the patter of water as it bounced off stones in a river hidden behind thick pines.

Joy jumped and squealed in fright when Gerhart burst through the trees.

He didn't first see the young girl, busying himself with removing clothes. His tunic lay open, barely hanging from his upper arms. What a racket he made while hopping on one foot; the other in his hands while he fought to remove his boot.

He fell, landing against a sturdy elm, before he looked up to see an angel standing nearby.

When Joy realized the frightening sounds originated from a man and not a wild animal, she relaxed, though her emotions did not. She changed from fright to anger.

Gerhart stared at the unexpected beauty glaring at him and grinned. It took seconds to kick off his boots and the rest of his clothes.

She stared in disbelief. Never had a common gypsy ever disrespected her so. She huffed and left the riverbank, never thinking of her safety.

Gerhart grinned at her retreating back. He shrugged before jumping into the water to wash several days of grime from his skin.

Joy returned home, breathless. Her mind refused to obey her command to forget the man at the river. She told herself she was too high-born to fall for such a rogue. Besides, she was betrothed to the lord of a nearby, rich land.

She told herself he was a rogue. He was both brazen and uncivilized. She closed her eyes tightly and tried thinking about anything but the handsome, naked gypsy.

Her father saw her red face and bothered expression and wondered the cause. When he asked, Joy opened her mouth to report the intruder, but still, her mind would not listen. Instead, she explained she had just run from the stream and merely felt weary from the exercise.

The Baron accepted her answer but scolded her for going off on her own and playing near the stream. He had lost another daughter at that same stream, years before. The bank, weak after heavy rains, fell away and she slipped. She hit her head on a stone and drowned.

Joy understood her father's worry. She missed her twin sister every day. She retired to her chambers to change her gown and rest. When she lay on her large, soft mattress, her thoughts returned to the man near the river.

Her memory fought to recall his tanned skin, his muscles, and his face. All she could see was his naked form. She had never seen a man in such a state before.

Exhausted but intrigued, her thoughts faded to dreams about the day's adventures.

She sat by the brook. Her feet hung over the bank, cooling in the mild current. Just down-stream, rocks changed the smooth water into a bubbling torrent. She leaned backward onto her arms and tilted her head, so the afternoon sun warmed her cheeks.

Suddenly, a wild boar broke through the brush and stopped. She jumped; a small squeak passed her lips. The boar didn't charge. Instead, it seemed to ignore her completely, jumping into the deepest part of the river and grunting happily.

When water splashed across her face in the dream, she woke. Her father knocked on the door moments later. He told her to dress and join him in the hall.

Joy, an obedient girl, did as her father commanded. Only moments later, she climbed the two steps to the dais where the Baron, her family, and honored guests sat.

Beside her father sat a man she knew well. He asked for Joy's hand years before she was old enough to accept. The Baron accepted the proposal, knowing his daughter would be well cared for. Joy liked the man well enough though she did not love him. She knew it was her duty and would not disobey her father. She smiled before sitting beside her betrothed.

Still, in the back of her mind, Joy's thoughts turned to the gypsy in the woods. She wondered who he could be. She knew she would not be permitted to wed such a man who could not keep her safe nor provide for her.

The Baron stood and thumped his silver mug on the table. The room immediately became silent as a prayer. His chest puffed outward in pride; his men knew their role.

After looking outward, he cleared his throat and announced that, to celebrate Joy coming of age to marry, he hired entertainment; a minstrel and gypsies to perform.

Joy felt her heart skip a beat at hearing her father's announcement. Would the wandering gypsy come? She felt her cheeks heat with a flush.

The guards, soldiers, guests, and nobles ate their fill. Jovial conversation and the occasional ale-fueled argument gave the crowd a lulled, sedate sense of contentment.

Joy, however, felt anxious. She silently prayed the gypsy from the stream would come through the door.

Her father noticed Joy's behavior and smirked. He didn't know her thoughts, thinking her apprehension and excitement proved he pleased her.

Believing Joy searched for entertainment, he waved for a servant to bring the troupe into the hall.

Joy's breath caught in her throat. She watched impatiently for jugglers, tumblers, fire-eaters, and musicians to enter and perform. She sat back, swallowing her disappointment, when the last of the entertainers crossed the threshold and the doors closed; the gypsy was not among them.

She politely watched, clapped at the end of every performance, but her heart wasn't in it. Joy stood to excuse herself when a commotion caught her attention.

The doors burst open; servants peered toward the dais. They feared repercussions from the Baron, but he only watched, intrigued; a lone figure in dingy-brown clothes entered, brazenly whistling as though his invitation had been for the high table! He looked directly at Joy, winking. The small, innocent act prompted her betrothed to sputter in frustration at the gypsy's audacity.

Joy reached over and patted his fist and smiled when he looked her way. The nobleman quickly calmed, soothed by her understanding glance.

The Baron addressed the gypsy who apologized for his lateness. He bowed again before beginning his routine. Light on his feet, he danced to the tune he whistled. Not once did he lose his breath though he took full advantage of the large hall's floor.

His happy tune made everyone smile and join in. Even Joy, the Baron, and guests whistled along.

Though the gypsy moved through the crowd, never did he forget to look toward the dais to see if the beautiful lady watched. His heart buzzed in his chest whenever he made eye-contact. He swore to himself he would win her heart and take her from this keep.

Finally, the evening turned to night, and the performers, servants, and soldiers left the hall.

They gypsy waved to the men and kissed the women's hands when they walked through the door. A few female servants giggled or gasped when he took their hands in his and bent to graze his lips across their skin.

He remained just outside the hall, listening to the noblemen scold Joy. He leaned against the wall, arms and ankles crossed. He waited, hoping to coax Joy into a late-night stroll around the grounds.

The Baron, Joy, and their guest left through a door near the dais. None saw the gypsy standing outside.

A young servant girl took pity on the handsome young gypsy several minutes later. She told him none remained in the hall when he asked.

Crestfallen, the gypsy stood upright, his hands falling to his sides. He kicked at a lump of dried mud left on the floor before leaving the keep. Undeterred, however, he resolved to stay nearby in the hopes of another chance.

From the Diaphragm

Sunlight woke the gypsy from a pleasant dream. He and Joy had spent the night together in a grand keep in a large bedchamber. Three children clambered onto the bed to jump and awaken them.

Everyone laughed and played until his rude awakening by God's celestial alarm. He stretched and rubbed his eyes before assessing his surroundings. Beasts of burden roamed nearby, enjoying sweet grass and flowers. Servants walked along paths from nearby villages, and serfs tilled the earth to plant early grains.

Joy tossed and turned the entire night. She dreamt of riding far away with the nobleman. He was unkind and reclusive. He did not beat her, but he wouldn't talk to her nor look at her when she spoke. Their marriage bed rested half-cold while he spent his nights with his soldiers, drinking and planning raids on nearby lands. She awoke with a start when the sun peeked through her window; the tapestries had not been pulled tightly closed the evening before. She thought to scold her chambermaid the moment she saw her.

Joy stumbled from her bed, nearly falling backward atop it when she lost her balance. Fresh water placed in a basin helped wash the sleep from her brain. She took a look in her long mirror and sighed. She clearly saw the results of her restless sleep in her tangled hair and bloodshot eyes.

Joy did her best to look presentable before joining her father for breakfast. He always scolded her if she did not appear rested and ready for the day.

When she reached the dais, she noticed, surprisingly, her betrothed had not yet left. She remembered he said he would leave in the night. She thought perhaps the moon did not adequately light the path.

Joy quickly finished breakfast, choosing fruit, bread, and milk, and left the table, bored with the conversation.

The grounds bustled with activity, energizing her spirit. She irrationally looked around for the gypsy, knowing he left with the others the previous night.

Joy thought of the last two dreams she'd had. One dream confused her, the other distressed. She sat on a low, wooden bench and closed her eyes. The sun warmed her face and gave her peace.

She jerked when someone barreled through the gates. Guards roared loudly at the mounted intruder. He rode straight for Joy and scooped her into his arms. She did not resist, too shocked by the suddenness of the act. Instead, she held onto the stranger, afraid she may fall and be trampled.

The gypsy directed the horse toward the gate. Guards, afraid they would hurt the lady, did little to stop them. The two rode unencumbered through the castle gates and away from the villages. The guards clamored to saddle horses to follow.

Joy continued to clutch the gypsy around the waist, her position unbalanced across his lap. Finally, when the horse cleared her father's land, the gypsy slowed to a halt and dismounted. He did not release his captured lady. Instead, he sat on a log, tugging her to his lap.

Joy didn't seem keen to remove herself nor return to her home. She resolved to abdicate her title, ignore her bloodline, and live the life of a roving gypsy. She rested her head against his shoulder and remained still.

The gypsy's heart fluttered. He smiled and hummed a song he had learned as a child. A traveling minstrel would sing of lords and ladies bound by duty instead of love. Ladies given to men they would not care for, yet they would not leave the riches of the lands. He vowed to find a woman to love him for himself.

He asked Joy her name and grinned when she told him. He rested a hand on his chest and told her she brought him immeasurable joy, making her smile.

Joy and the gypsy rode for hours, talking about their dreams and hopes.

They reached a grand castle. The double curtain walls held iron gates, guard posts, and a busy bailey inside.

The Baron finished reprimanding his guards for allowing the rider to take his daughter. The nobleman stood nearby, grumbling under his breath.

They mounted and rode through the gate in the direction the guards indicated. The rider had a head start, but two rode the horse, slowing escape.

They rode throughout the countryside, breaking into three groups to cover more ground. Many hours went by; the Baron felt more afraid for his daughter's safety every moment. He rode through villages, asking at inns and taverns. None had seen the riders.

The moon crested and the sun set before the Baron heard hopeful news. Someone told him of a horse running quickly through the village with two people mounted. The villager pointed toward a large castle that could be seen from miles away. He mentioned his lord, but the baron ignored his warning.

The Baron rewarded the villager with a few silver coins and rode quickly to the east and prayed he would find his daughter safe and sound.

Darkness met the Baron by the time he reached the castle's closed gates. He shouted to the guards, demanding entry.

The guards refused. Their lord had given the command to not open the gates after the sun fell below the horizon.

The Baron tried threats, his title, his daughter's kidnapping; none swayed their resolve.

Suddenly, the Baron stopped shouting. Joy stood far away, behind the gates, glowing with happiness. She wore a shimmering, golden gown. Someone had braded her hair with yellow blooms and ribbons. She looked like a goddess. She approached the gate and smiled at her father. His eyes watered, his mouth agape at the sight before his eyes.

She told him the gypsy was not a poor rover as they had both believed. Instead, he was a rich lord with many holdings. He had spent his time roaming the countryside looking for a woman who would love him without his money and believed he had found such a woman in Joy.

She told her father she loved the man and would break her betrothal to stay with him. She vowed to never leave the man who stole her heart with a whistle and a wink.

Saxon Bryce

Harden My Heart

"Meet me, baby. I'ma gonna be a little late but I promise. This time, I'll be there."

Katherine didn't trust Jameil. He always let her down, but she loved him and wanted to believe he wouldn't stand her up this time. "Alright. I'll be there. Our corner. You best be there this time, or I swear, I'll..."

"Jameil stood tall and loomed over Katherine. "Or, you'll what?"

Intimidated by his threatening voice, Kat cowered. "Nothing."

"S'what I thought. A'ight, I gotta go. Bye for now, baby."

Kat gave him a kiss. He possessively squeezed her butt and left her in front of the market where she worked.

Jameil took off in a low-rider with his friends. Josue drove, Christian shotgun. Jameil rode in back with Tre. "Yo! What's crack-a-lackin'?"

Josue reached over the seat, palm out. Tre put a Pabst beer in his open hand.

The friends laughed and cracked jokes while riding down the city streets. Up to little good, they searched sidewalks for their next victim.

***

"Kat don't forget to restock the Snickers. They've been low for a bit, now."

"Okay, Mr. Keith. I'll do it now. "Kat walked to the storage room at the back of the store and grabbed three boxes of the popular treat. She put them on a cart and rolled it to the check-out aisles. Mr. Keith, the owner, thought safety first and set rules to reduce incidents. That included never carrying inventory. Even the lightest weight and smallest sized containers would be placed on a cart to transport. Kat thought it was a silly rule, but Mr. Keith was a nice man and she would humor him. She looked at the clock; two more hours.

***

Jameil and his friends spotted someone they thought would be an easy mark. A middle-aged woman walked alone. She held a purse, a shopping bag, and a cane.

"She ain't hardly worth the trouble."

Tre laughed at Josue's insult. "Kinda takes the fun out, huh?"

His buddies agreed and they continued, looking for a bigger challenge.

"Look at dat!" Christian yelled. Two well-dressed college boys walked down the street. "I ain't never seen no men holdin' hands like dat, before," he continued.

"Christian, man! This be the age of everyone doin' their thang, son! Get wit da times."

Tre felt uncomfortable. He knew his attraction to men was natural for him. He just wasn't sure how his buddies would react, so he hadn't come out to them, yet.

"Yeah, yeah. I know. Ain't just never seen it is all."

Jameil, wise enough to know Tre's secret, changed the subject to their plans. "Look easy mark?"

"Naw. They fit. I say we take 'em." Josue pulled his car to the curb and parked.

***

Kat looked at the clock. One more hour, and she would leave work and walk to the corner where she and Jameil first met. They called it their corner.

Many times, Kat often stood on that corner, rain or shine, waiting for Jameil. Sometimes, he would come late. Sometimes, he would not show at all. She vowed repeatedly, she would give him only one more chance, but he would convince her, time and again, to forgive him.

She looked outside; rain fell against the concrete, pattering on the kelly-green awning that shaded the store on sunny days.

"That don't look good, Kat. Want me to give you a lift somewhere when you get off?"

Kat looked appreciatively at her boss. She nearly took him up on his offer but changed her mind. "No thanks, Mr. Keith. It'll probably stop by the time we close up, anyway."

"Okie dokey. Let me know if you change your mind."

"I will. Thanks, again."

The pair returned to their tasks as the rain pelted down, punishing the streets.

***

Jameil, Tre, Josue, and Christian followed the couple down the street. They kept their distance, biding their time. The couple sensed imminent threat and walked faster to create distance between themselves and the quartet who followed.

Jameil seemed to sense their fear and went into hunter versus prey mode. "I think dey scared."

Tre chuckled nervously. He no longer wished to play the game with the couple ahead. "I...I don't know, guys. What if one of 'em knows karate or some shit?"

"Losing your nerve, little Tre? Need you mama, baby Tre?"

Tre lost his temper and shouted at his friends. "You think I lost my nerve? Watch this!"

At that moment, the sky rumbled, and clouds blew together. Thunder clapped and lightning lit the sky. Quickly, occasional raindrops changed to a light-stealing torrent.

"Jesus. This ain't good. Abort da mission, crew!"

Tre, determined to prove himself, stormed forward to the students who took shelter in a covered doorway. Distracted by the rain and each other, they didn't see Tre approach until he stood directly in front of them.

"Your wallets."

They stared at the knife and didn't hear his words.

"Your wallets or one of you is dyin' tonight. Hell might be both you."

The threat brought them back to the dire situation. "Wallets, right. Sweetie, get your wallet and give it to the nice man."

Tre scoffed. He longed to call someone 'sweetie' but couldn't take the chance.

Josue, Christian, and Jameil watched from a nearby awning. They would never have taken such a risk in the bad weather. "Guess we riled 'im?"

"Maybe a little."

Tre's hands shook. He was cold, wet, and afraid. His friends stood too far away to help, and he knew better than to rob people when it'd be harder to get away.

He reached up to wipe water from his eyes. That slight gesture enough for one of his victims to reach forward, grab the blade, and thrust it into Tre's collar. His partner shrieked.

"Blood. Look at it! It's ruining your pants."

The man who stabbed Tre grabbed the other's hand and ran from under the awning.

Tre dropped to his knees and looked at his friends, reaching out, begging for help.

Christian ran toward Tre; Josue left, driving away in his car.

Jameil stared at the surreal scene. Everything seemed to go in slow motion. He looked from the retreating Josue, to the victims-turned-killers, to Tre bleeding onto the concrete. The blood streamed from the sidewalk into a storm grate.

His head spun. He'd never seen so much blood. Christian knelt beside the now-prone Tre, crying and pleading for Tre to stay awake.

Tre's eyes rolled into his head. Christian pushed against the wound, trying to stop the flow. He kept talking to Tre. The injured man opened his eyes and reached to wipe rain and tears from his friend's face.

Jamail's world righted. He looked at what looked more like a couple than just friends and shook his head before turning away.

***

Kat stood in the door. She watched the relentless rain pummel the ground. Hungry grass and leaves drank their fill but most spilled onto the concrete.

"Sure you don't want that ride? I don't mind, ya know."

"It's nice you offered, but I'll be okay."

"I'll see you tomorrow, then?"

"You betcha!" Kat loved the hokey way her boss talked and began using her favorite phrases.

They left the shop, Mr. Keith locked the door, and they said their good-byes. She turned west and started walking toward the corner. She smiled. Kat always believed rain washed away all the bad and left the world shiny and new. She hummed a little song while she kicked at rocks and splashed in puddles, giggling when a few drops would roll down her back, tickling her skin.

Finally, she reached the corner. The rain refused to relent. Kat started singing songs about rain. She knew Jameil might not show up, but this time, he'd promised. "He'll be here. He has to. If he doesn't, sorry, heart, I gotta move on. Ain't got no more room for yo lies, Jameil."

Kat stood on the corner. Rain fell without mercy, pasting her clothes to her curves. Her hair, once a bounty of loose curls, now clung to her face and neck.

Water ran into her eyes. She no longer giggled when droplets caressed her skin. She felt the sting of tears, lessened by dilution from the raindrops.

Kat took a deep breath, swallowed the lump in her throat, and closed her eyes. She willed herself to harden her heart and walk away.

She left the corner and walked down the street. Her phone rested atop the Walk/Don't Walk light.

***

Jameil still ran. He forgot Kat. He forgot his promise. He saw red, blood blinding his eyes and clouding his thoughts.

He didn't mean to lie to Kat, but he intuitively knew she was no longer his girl. He felt a tear before he hardened his own heart against the pain.

From the Diaphragm

Willie McBride

I heard the drums slowly pounding a mournful tune. Whispering along, fifes sang their sorrow out into the world. I stood in the center of the ancient cemetery. A stone rested deep in the mud. I knelt to wash a century of dirt from the crevasses that spelled out a name and year of death.

I reached for a dowel. It looked like someone may have snapped it from a small flag. The dirt began to give way from the etchings as I scratched at the stone.

The arduous task took over an hour, but the results bore fruit. I stood, wiped the dirt from my knees and hands, and looked upon the gravestone.

"Well, how do you do?" I stared at the young man's name, Willie McBride. I threw my jacket on the ground and sat beside him.

Somehow, I thought this boy, nineteen years when they laid him to rest, deserved a story. Between the two of us, I felt we could spin a tale of sorrow and love.

I paused, looked around at all the white crosses covering the land surrounding me. I had walked many miles before reaching this, my current destination. I had come across a funeral procession along the way, though I didn't know the deceased. I, instead, walked on, finding my silent companion, far from the new burials on the other side of the hill.

Tell me, Willie, did you die quickly? Were you in the war? Did you even want to fight? You aren't French. Was it hard to leave home?" I received no reply, as expected, but Willie's stone and cross gave me very little to go on.

I laid on the ground and closed my eyes, imagining the young man's face. I vividly saw bright-blue eyes, sandy-red hair, and a playful, crooked grin. I envisioned a boyish face above a willowy frame, barely strong enough to wield a rifle.

He held a beautiful young woman in his arms. She wept silently while he stroked her hair. I heard the girl's worry in her words and his assurances of a safe return.

Upon closer inspection, I noticed the man wore trousers bloused at the top of shining, black boots. His jacket pressed, and his hat tilted to the left, a uniform cap.

The young man released his girl, kissed her on the forehead, picked up a rifle, and walked away.

He glanced, only once, to see the girl on her knees, sobbing and clasping her body with her arms, rocking as tears fell to the earth. She would love the young man for all time.

A boat carried the young man to the east. Willie sat quietly clutching a small, floral and lace cloth in one hand; in the other, he held a photograph I could only just see of the young girl and him. He ran a finger across the girl's image before tucking both items into a pocket. Someone had shouted a command, and Willie and his mates stood in formation, preparing to debark.

The sun shone hot on their backs as they faced east and nearby battles. Willie took a trembling breath, pulled his shoulders back, and followed the man at the front; lockstep and in time, just the way they had been trained.

They disembarked and returned to their positions within the platoon. More orders barked at them, informing each of their duties now they were on land.

The red-headed Willie followed many young men toward a pile of canvas and wooden poles. They paired off and worked to construct housing and medical tents.

Willie's partner complained throughout the chore. He expected to go to war and kill the enemy. Willie smirked, winked, and nodded his head toward two others digging a trench. He seemed to indicate things could be worse and continued their task, putting only a few feet between each temporary structure.

I opened my eyes and looked up at a cloud. It looked, when I squinted, like a face. One eye peered downward, the other nothing more than a slit. I knew my new friend, Willie, smiled and winked at me. I returned the expression before returning to the tale playing in my mind. I paused a moment, hoping I did Willie's tale justice.

Dinnertime, a welcome respite from the day's chores. Dirt-stained and exhausted, the men lined up by rank. Willie and half his platoon stood at the front of the line. Lowest ranks did most of the work, got paid the least, but they ate before the rest. This tradition surprised Willie, but it was a pleasant surprise.

My visions blurred. Faces and the encampment spun. A conundrum of brown and green whirled, muddy and sad. I squeezed my eyes tight, willing my story to refocus.

Finally, a loud sound, perhaps nearby, perhaps just in my mind, caused my story to return focus. Red filtered my vision; Willie looked to his left just to close his own eyes as blood and brains caked his face and neck. The man who had just moments before killed four enemy soldiers stood beside him, face and half his skull gone.

It took what seemed an eternity for his body to realize he was dead. Another enemy fell after muscle memory kicked in, and one final, deadly shot rang out from the dead man's M-14.

The battle raged on. My deceased friend fought valiantly. He screamed or shouted angrily when an Irishman would fall and cheered when another German soldier's rifle fell silent. He hid behind the rare tree or laid on his stomach, perched on his elbows. He reloaded twice before he felt a pinch then searing heat tear through his shoulder, exiting at the base of his ribs.

Tears streaked his cheeks but not from pain. Willie knew, if he died, he would never see his beautiful girl again. He cried for the loss of so many of his brothers. He cried in fear of his lands becoming something else. If they did not hold the tyrants to these shores, they would, most assuredly, continue forward toward England, Wales, and Scotland, taking them over before another short jaunt to bonny Eire.

I felt something skitter across my cheekbone. I reached up to swipe the intruder away but realized my cheeks were wet with tears. I sat, took many cleansing breaths, and collected my composure. I told myself it was only a story I made up to view another's life. It was not real.

After allowing the humid sunshine to warm my skin and dry my tears, I stood, put my hand on Willie McBride's grave marker, to say farewell. An odd pull tugged at my heart and I sat, again, hoping to relieve the sensation.

Instead, a graphic image materialized before my eyes. A scene from history; the battle ended. Blood soaked the ground, sending the souls of the damned to their permanent homes in Hell.

Willie laid face-down on the muddy field, writhing in physical pain and emotional agony. In his hand, he held a photograph. It trembled with his dying spirit. He closed his eyes, clutched a crucifix hidden beneath his blouse, and begged God to find him home.

Men with a stretcher walked up to Willie and myriad fallen soldiers laying around him. One kicked dead men's boots; each recipient motionless. He would cut their dog tags from their boot laces or tug them until the chain snapped from around each neck. He put the tags into a man's mouth and slammed the jaws tight to lodge the identity of each man to notify next of kin when the boys returned home.

Willie groaned and pulled his leg away when kicked. The soldier shouted something to his partner who had walked away. It disturbed him, the things they had to do to these poor, unfortunate young men.

A stretcher held Willie and the men carried his small, bleeding, dying body to a large truck. He joined many others who groaned, cried, wailed, or merely lay still, staring at the canvas cover protecting them from the brutal sun.

I felt physical pain as I watched the horrific scene unfold before my eyes. So many young men dead. Others permanently changed, forever. I knew in my heart, Willie would die.

I wondered if he would make it home first, or would he die in a makeshift hospital; a tent with bleached canvas and a large, red cross on the roof? Would he have a chance to say goodbye?

I got my answer soon enough. Willie, naked to the waist, lay on a table. The poor lighting told me I looked at a field hospital. Three men stood over him. They cut his torso from entry to exit. After what seemed an eternity, Willie's eyes opened. His lifeless face gave me a moment's pause. I watched him die as though I stood in the operating tent at his side.

My breath caught before returning with difficulty. I wept for the loss of a man I never knew. The image returned to my moment.

From the Diaphragm

I stared at Willie's marker, lost in silent prayer. I turned to resume my travels and bumped into an elderly woman. She looked curiously at me then Willie's marker.

My mind raced. Was this Willie's lover from 1916? She looked the right age. I cleared my throat, hoping to speak with a steady tone.

I asked the woman if she knew Willie. She gave me a sad smile and nodded. Again, she diverted her eyes toward the grave.

Intuitively, I knew her to be the woman from my tale. She began to speak. Her voice warm and rich, her tale completed my story.

The story I imagined came to life again. She told me of the teary goodbye, of the ship taking her young man to France to fight the great war. She told me stories she had been told of how he fought valiantly, just to die on a table in a dimly lit hospital tent, and how she regretted, every day since, that she had not the opportunity to know the man he could have become.

When I left the grieving woman at Willie McBride's grave, I wondered if he wanted his story told so he could live on when his woman passed from the earth.

I will never know, but I will never forget the brief glimpse Willie McBride gave me into his life's end.

Saxon Bryce

Careless Whisper

"I'm sorry."

"How could you do that to me?"

"I said I'm sorry! Please stay?"

Michael literally dropped to his knees. His partner loomed above, arms crossed, angry, sad tears poured from his eyes.

"How can I ever trust you, Michael?"

Michael wondered how Jimmy heard about what he'd done. Though only a dance, the night could have ended easily with him following the stranger home from the dance floor. Who told Jimmy of the sexy dance, the roaming hands, the too-close bodies?

"How..."

"Does it matter, Michael?"

Michael flinched. James Randolph Boone only used his Christian name when he had been hurt emotionally. "I suppose it doesn't."

Jimmy reached down to clutch the handle on his hot-pink suitcase and rolled it to the door, his heart breaking.

"I'm not going to do it again!"

Jimmy paused, hand on the door handle, thumb on the latch. "Do what, exactly?"

Michael froze; his voice caught in his throat. He didn't know how to answer the direct question laced with angst and pain. He cleared his throat to delay and collect his thoughts. Finally, he found his voice, "Dance."

Jimmy spun around so fast his cases teetered and he had to lean against the door to keep from falling over. "Dance. You won't dance anymore. Precious, that is not what this is about."

Michael winced again. Jimmy's term of endearment cut with the precision of a surgeon's scalpel. He didn't know what else to say so he threw his hands into the air and shouted angrily as though he was the wronged party.

"That's what I thought." Jimmy huffed and turned back to the door. It clicked with finality behind him.

Michael collapsed. His heart constricted and he fell forward; his head and forearms against the floor. He sobbed into the puce-colored shag area rug Jimmy insisted on buying. He remembered telling Michael it looked snazzy with the chartreuse accent wall.

Tears dried only after hours. Michael lifted his weary body from the floor and washed his swollen eyes and face at the bathroom sink.

Jimmy had been Michael's best friend since they started school over twenty years before. Before either knew they did not have normal attractions. Before they had any attractions at all.

Now, at twenty-seven, Michael knew his idle hands had ruined their future together. He walked to the room he shared with his lover and fell onto the bed. Two rows of ornamental pillows jumped up and off their perch when the overstuffed comforter puffed and released a thrust of air after impact. Michael could not be moved to care.

"Never again. God, bring him back to me. I can't go on without him. Please?" Michael prayed to an entity he didn't believe in. He prayed Jimmy would forgive him.

Jimmy returned to the empty apartment three days later. He stayed with a friend—Margaret. Before he'd left the complex, he'd asked a neighbor to call him when he knew Michael was not in the flat.

He opened the door and entered. Margaret followed, dragging a stack of bins on a flatbed cart. "Where ya wanna start?"

Jimmy sighed. He loved Michael. Thanks to his friends' advice, he resolved to love and respect himself, first. He shrugged, his head moving from side to side. "I guess we can start in the bedroom and work toward the door."

"Got it. Operation 'Free Jimmy' will commence in the back. Lead on, boss-man."

Jimmy giggled. He truly appreciated his best girlfriend he lovingly called 'Mag-Hag'. She could always get him to laugh.

It took two bins for just the bed pillows, alone. Jimmy huffed, annoyed to find the bed disheveled, pillows on the floor. "It's like he slept on top of everything!"

Margaret let him rant while she filled bins with sequined jackets, shining trousers, delicate 'manties', and nylon stockings. She had always appreciated Jimmy's style. "Hey, do you have a big trash bag?"

"Yeah, in the...wait! Why?"

"Wanted to cut a hole in one and slip it over your hanging clothes. I don't want to mess them up by putting 'em into bins."

"Always taking care of me."

"You know it!"

Jimmy heard of Michael's antics through a mutual friend. Bruce Evans was Michael's confidant...the person he told all his secrets to. Jimmy overheard Bruce whispering, carelessly loudly, about Michael dancing with a man at the club. He laughed about how the stranger would pull him close and how he seemed to want to take him right there on the dance floor. Jimmy sat two tables away. He tried minding his business until Bruce mentioned one name—Michael.

"Okay. All done, honey, what's next?"

Jimmy grabbed a bin from the stack. "I'll do the bathroom. You wanna do the kitchen? If it's colorful, it's mine."

He went to the bathroom and put the bin on the closed toilet lid. He smiled a little. It had taken him four years to train Michael to shut the ring and another two to close the lid.

After towels, robe, toiletries, cologne, and moisturizers, Jimmy rolled the bath rugs and padded the bin contents to reduce rattling. He struggled to carry the heavy bin to the cart.

Jimmy looked around his apartment. It spoke volumes about Michael. Though the room screamed flamboyance, Jimmy's style, Michael had spent years in a world in which he felt a stranger. "No wonder!"

"What was that?" Margaret walked in from the kitchen with a full bin.

"Nothing, sweetie. I was just thinking out loud."

Margaret twisted her lips and eyed Jimmy. She could look right through him and knew there was more to his outburst. However, she knew he was still trying to come to terms with his new life. "Okay." She didn't press.

"Well..."

Margaret paused and looked at Jimmy. Clearly, he had something on his mind.

"It's just..."

"Hmm?" She stopped moving after grabbing another bin.

"I am so selfish!" Jimmy finally got his thoughts into the air.

Margaret could see her friend's resolve wavering and chose to intervene. "Jimmy, remember what he did."

"Yeah, but..."

"No. You don't need to do this, now. Come on. Let's take this stuff back to my place. We can get the rest later."

"But, I mean, it's Michael. He and I have been thick as thieves forever!"

Margaret's only chance to keep Jimmy from unpacking and returning to the toxicity of Michael's overbearing need to be in control came quickly.

"Come on. Help me." Jimmy leaned over and grabbed a bin. "I don't want to take everything. He won't have anything. I bought all this to make our..."

"Not yours, Jimmy. Michael's."

Jimmy pouted, flourished his arms, and dropped onto the custom-made floral Victorian chaise lounge chair. "I can't do this, Mag-Hag. I can't leave him."

Margaret swallowed a growl. The last thing Jimmy needed was another overbearing, bossy influence telling him what to do. She sat at his side and tucked her arm around his frail shoulders. She took a deep breath and softened her voice. "Jimmy, honey..."

"Don't you honey me, Margaret. My mind is made..."

The door slammed shut. Michael glared at Jimmy and Margaret. "What's all this?" He gestured at the bins packed on the cart.

"It's not what you..."

Margaret interrupted Jimmy's apology. "He's leaving you, Michael."

Jimmy stared, wide-eyed. Michael's usually neatly combed hair stuck out at angles. His eyes, bloodshot, rested in dark circles surrounding his eyes. His clothes were wrinkled beyond repair. Michael's shoulders drooped and he looked at the floor. The man looked nothing like the self-assured, confident, consummate professional Jimmy had grown to love.

"Mikey?" His voice higher than usual, his tone concerned.

Michael looked hopefully at his best friend and former lover. His eyes, wet with tears, pleaded for another chance.

Margaret stood and put her hand out to take Jimmy's. He reluctantly took her hand and stood. She guided him gently to the door. Before opening it, Jimmy turned to look at Michael's back. "Goodbye, Mike."

Michael walked to his bedroom, refusing to speak. Margaret nodded toward the bedroom and gave Jimmy a 'I told you so' look. Jimmy nodded and opened the door. She rolled the cart through and Jimmy pulled his keys from his pocket, removed the key to the lock, and put it on a small table near the door. "Goodbye, Mikey," he whispered into the room and closed the door.

As Margaret drove off, Jimmy looked toward his home of six years and silently cried.

Michael stood in the window and watched the love of his life, his best friend, leave him. He walked to the bathroom and took a prescription bottle from the shelf. A loud pop, the rattle of pills, the rush of tap water. He took them all, tossed his head back, swallowed with difficulty, and returned to his now-stripped bed.

"What I did. So wrong. So wrong. Now you've left me. I'm alone."

The last words Michael uttered before falling into a

From the Diaphragm

permanent sleep, "I'm sorry."

Saxon Bryce

Home from the Sea

The unforgiving waves thrust the small fishing boat across the four-foot waves. Men lashed themselves to masts and rails, praying for help. The mainsail rested, limp and useless, floating folded and drenched in the foam.

"Captain! Didja get ahold o' the rescue boats? We can't come in without the mainsail. We're dead if you can't."

"I know my job, Charlie. I called 'em. Said they'd be coming to get us. Tie yourself on, son."

Charlie, first-mate on the small fishing boat, opened his mouth to argue, but he changed his mind when he saw the worry on the captain's face. "Aye, Captain."

The rescue squad looked for brave men to volunteer. Many men refused to go, fearing their own early demise.

"God'll take ya on land if He's going to take ya. He will keep ya safe it ain't your time to go."

Finally, six young men came forward. "We'll go. Die if we must, but we're ready to help."

Women, old men, and children lined the road that led to the harbor wall. Each kept silent vigil, the storm slashing banners, gowns, and streets; a relentless and non-discriminant assailant.

Finally, the lifeboat left the harbor. All aboard feared the worst. The small vessel pitched and tossed.

Torrential rain and deadly waves threatened the volunteers' safety. Though every man feared his own death, the words of the harbormaster resonated like a soothing song on their minds.

"God won't take us unless it's our time," a volunteer spoke the words they all thought.

The fishing vessel cracked, threatening to break. It held together with sheer will. The captain tried calling the harbormaster again, but a large wave caused his boat to list. The radio antennae snapped, swallowed by the sea. Nobody could call.

"Light the torch, Charlie. Vincent, tie yourself to something else. The wind's 'bout to take that mast. Jonesy stop your caterwauling. You're a grown-assed man."

Charlie spent the better part of ten minutes trying to get the flint spark to ignite the waterlogged oil wick. Finally, the spark caught the wick and began to burn. Quickly, before the rain extinguished the fledgling flame, he clicked the glass door shut and turned the wick to brighten the night sky.

The captain returned to the wheelhouse and closed the door. Two windows, cracked when the boat twisted in the waves, gave way, shattering inward, cutting the captain's cheek. Blood flowed freely, encouraged by the continuous influx of rain into the breached cabin. He cursed but didn't try to stop the flow.

Charlie, tied to a solid-iron pole, watched the alarm flame flicker. He prayed the wick was long enough, that the lamp would not break, that someone would come quickly and save them before any died and fell to the depths of the great ocean, joining fishermen long dead.

The lifeboat, still visible from the harbor wall, struggled in the pitch-black, stormy sea. They had a mission to complete and would finish it.

"No turning back, now, boys. Best keep praying. I can't see anything out here! Keep your eyes on the sea. Look for a sign of that fishing boat."

"We can't see, either, Captain." Everyone felt the fear, palpable like a living, breathing beast in the night.

"Home, God. Carry us home. Merciful angels help guide us. We're begging you. Help us." The fishing boat crew cried into the night. No stars showed their position. No moon lit the sky. The storm clouds blackened the night and the crew's spirit.

The captain wiped rain and blood from his eyes and prayed a rescue came soon. Another mast, the one Vincent moved from, cracked under the strain and broke away, taking a length of rail and a section of the bow with it to a watery grave.

The lantern on the deck glowed an eerie gold. Charlie kept vigilant watch over the crew. Three, four, five, seven. All men accounted for. He closed his eyes and thanked the gods for their protection.

Finally, the lifeboat crossed from the bay, meeting more waves and danger in the open sea. Each volunteer thought of the people they'd left behind. Wives, mothers, and children stayed behind. Every man prayed they would see them again.

The vessel valiantly battled the waves. Everyone kept their heads clear, their eyes outward. The volunteer crew strained to find any sign of life.

"Look there! Is that a light?"

Others looked in the direction the man pointed. No one else saw the light. The man who shouted felt betrayed by his very eyes and looked downward, his over-long hair falling, drenched into his eyes. He couldn't be bothered to wipe it away.

"There it is! I see it, too!"

Everyone began to cheer and shout. The fishing boat floated lifeless in the water, but the rescuers felt certain some must have survived. The lifeboat hurried toward the other vessel. It tossed and listed, nobody seemed to steer.

"Captain, what do you see?"

"I see something, Charlie. I think it's a boat. We're saved, son. How many have we lost?" The captain feared Charlie's reply. He could not see the deck from his perch.

"Not a one, Captain. All alive and accounted."

The captain's heart felt light. The gods of the sea may have tried, but none would be taken today.

The men cheered after the captain's words and Charlie's report. All would go home.

The muddy gravel street, filled now with the village's entire population, stood together. None could see the lifeboat nor the fishing ship. Their hearts sunk with worry. It took too long. Something must be wrong. They feared the storm was too much for the lifeboat, for the fishermen.

"They're gone, folks. Nobody could'a survived that." The harbormaster's words cut through the waning storm. It had moved out to sea, heading right for the fishing boat's reported coordinates.

Pairs of wives, lovers, and concerned villagers stood at the base of the stairs leading to the harbor. They held each other's trembling hands and cried. None could tear away, just in case the harbormaster proved to be wrong.

A low sound caught their attention. Static on the radio. "Come again? There is interference."

"All survivors aboard. We're bringing them home." The captain's voice rang through the harbor like the song of angels on high.

The harbor lit with lanterns and candles, flashlights and sound. Everyone calling their loved-one's home.

Fiddler's Green

We shivered, standing on a ship not far from Greenland's western shore. The name of the island an ironic jest. Only rocks, boulders, sand, and ice to be seen. Though I am certain, at times, the grass grows abundant, I have never personally witnessed its glorious sight.

One of us, an elderly gent, a seasoned fisherman, sang a tune I thought sad and out of place. The haddock abundant, lobster and scallops in great multitude in our icy holds.

He sang of leaving. Asked many to wrap him tightly in his oilskin to stay dry and his jumper to stay warm. He vowed to meet us when we were ready to cross over.

I did not love the words though the song rang beautiful and melodic across the blood and sea water staining the deck. I slipped twice on a discarded haddock. It had seen too much battle. Damaged by swordfish to the point I felt sad yet amazed the fish had survived battle just to die, drowning on the floor.

The old fisherman, a friend to us all, played his accordion and sang. He sang of Fiddler's Green, a land of every desire. Heaven, I suppose, for those of the faith. Me? I'm riding the railings between yes and not. Perhaps there is a single being named God, perhaps many hold the title. Perhaps there is nothing after. We die, we're gone.

He continues. Fiddler's Green sounds like a right bonny place. Temperate climate, clear, blue skies, all welcoming and warm. He sang one could lay on the grass and watch dolphins play in the water.

I closed my eyes and listened to the deep timbre of our old fisherman's voice. I could almost feel the breeze. Never a gale around.

The tune continued. I stood on the deck of a perfect vessel. The fish, compliant, would just jump aboard, swishing their tails. Nobody needed to lift a finger nor lend a hand. I would love to see that!

Ha! He said the captain serves the crew tea he made in the galley. Now, that is certainly a land of dreams or fantasy. I chuckled and looked to the captain standing on the upper deck. He looked sad. I know he and our minstrel fisherman served on this very ship for decades. I suppose he would miss him.

The fishing boat made dock. I wanted to hear how this Fiddler's Green would look ashore. The fishermen all paused, now, in their duties, mesmerized by the song.

Of course! Pubs, clubs, and girls. Every sailor's dream after long days on the sea. Pretty girls, at that. I do like to gaze upon a pretty face, especially if that face is attached to a girl delivering flagon after flagon of beer and rum. What a life that would be!

I listened, I imagined, I hoped his words rang true. What a perfect place, this Fiddler's Green.

From the Diaphragm

He finished his song, making me feel sad once more. He hoped to die soon, be dressed warm and dry, and put out to sea to be carried away from Hell, but not toward Heaven. Maybe Fiddler's Green is a fisherman's Heaven.

He wanted no harm, no halo, no angels. All he asked was an accordion, riding the waves, and listening to the wind whistle through the riggings. He was ready to go.

I shed a tear. We would miss the old fisherman.

He stopped singing, the accordion silent. I opened my eyes and watched him drink from a tarnished flask. The fisherman, our friend, wiped his mouth on the back of his hand, winked at me, waved a salute to the captain. He closed his eyes with a smile and met his old fisher mates who had gone before him, to Fiddler's Green.

Saxon Bryce

Maid of Culmore

I had no choice. Caused to leave my beloved Derry County, my Culmore, to visit London, I stared at the harbor while floating to the east.

Children ran the streets, playing and squealing in glee. They would run to the shore and docks to see off the departing vessels and greet the ones that would come from England, Scotland, and Wales.

Each evening, bells would ring their joyous melody for only one—the Maid of Culmore.

Nobody could compare to the beautiful lass; she carried herself above others. I chanced to see her barely thrice before I left Culmore.

The first time I saw her, she didn't even see me though she looked directly at me. I smiled and waved but she merely turned her head; I was of no consequence to that perfect specter.

I thought myself fortunate to be graced with her image again several weeks later; this time, she did not ignore me but only bade me 'farewell'. I cannot even know why she would look sadly at me when she said it, but within a few moments, she was away again. I began to truly believe her a spirit or ghost; a person beyond my reach and beyond my understanding.

I would go to the Culmore's docks often. The children would always be there, playing and dancing at the water's edge. The Maid of Culmore didn't show again.

I began to think I'd imagined her standing on the docks near the beaches of Culmore. I believed I must have made her up.

Her beautiful chestnut brown hair and delicate freckles across her nose compelled me to keep coming; Culmore docks in the county Derry; the maid's essence called to me.

I spent restless nights tossing and turning. When sleep finally took me, I would dream. The Maid of Culmore invaded, kissed me sweetly just to disappear with the next breath. She teased me in my dreams and evaded me in my waking hours.

I avoided the docks, afraid I would see her again, afraid I would not. Neither would escape my mind.

Storms raged through the winter; the children still ran to the shores, oblivious to the freezing rain slamming the shore and ripping through their clothes. They had other things on their mind.

The bells rang as they always did. They rang to welcome ships in and say goodbye to those departing Culmore's shore.

I couldn't bear it one moment longer. I ran to the shore one last time. I had to know. Would I see her? Would she see me, or would she see through me? Was I, perhaps, the specter?

I stepped upon a ship sailing toward America. I had no intention of going, I merely wished to see from a different vantage.

On a neighboring vessel, staring directly at me, the Maid of Culmore. She stood there, waving. I knew by the expression across her face, I would never see her, again. I wanted to disembark, but the sailors readied the ship for transport and stood in my way. The ship on the port side sailed, the Maid of Culmore aboard.

I returned to my home, forlorn and aggrieved. The woman I dreamt of, the woman who loved me in my dreams, would be seen no more.

I laid in bed every night, praying storms would rage and bring her to me. I prayed wind and waves would return her to my view.

The prayers never answered, I boarded a ship, months later. The very ship I stood upon when I last saw the maiden. I prayed again, this time to ask God to bring me safely to the shores of America where I would search the continent for my love, the maiden I'd never see again.

Nobody will know me there; nobody will pay me heed. They will leave me to my own world, searching for the woman who stole my heart and sailed away to another land.

I know, if I don't find her, there will be no returning to my bonny Ireland. County Derry and Culmore will feel my footsteps no longer. I will walk the shores, travel across the lands, search north and south for my maiden. I will become a pilgrim and my pilgrimage will be in search of peace which I will only find once the Maid of Culmore rests her head on my shoulder and

From the Diaphragm

wraps her arms around my waist.
     It is my fate, my mission, my desire, and my life, to
find the Maid of Culmore or die in trying.

Saxon Bryce

Big, Bad John

"Get a load of that guy! He's a mountain!"

"That's John. He's the nicest guy you'll ever meet."

"I don't know, Jer. He looks intimidating as hell."

"Don't let looks fool you, Tom. He's a good one. Remember Nancy?"

"Nancy Pettyjohn?"

"Yeah, her."

"She's a bitch. Why you bring her up?"

"She looks pretty as a peach, doesn't she? She looked like a sweetheart, didn't she?"

Tom nodded.

"And then she started talking and behaving the way she does. I agree. She's a bitch. A right, nasty piece of work in a pretty package."

"I get your point, Jerry. So, he's a nice guy."

"Uh huh. Come on. Grab your hardhat. We gotta get to work."

"I hate this damn job. Mary wants me to quit but there isn't anything else for a man without skills to do."

"Yeah, Virginia is sure full of coal, though."

"It is for sure!"

Jerry and Tom rode the rail car into the mine. Tom watched the cross beams and the support beams. They vibrated along with the tracks below.

"This is damn dangerous."

"We can't think like that, Tom, or we'll be stuck here

doing a job we're scared of. Just get those thoughts out of your head."

Tom accepted Jerry's advice, but that wouldn't stop him from being afraid of a cave in.

The small rail car stopped about a mile below the surface. The miners poured out of the cars; John took up one by himself, his knees bent tight, his heels pushing against his bottom.

John never complained. He pushed and pushed until he could dislodge his massive frame from the small car. He leaned inside and grabbed a huge pickaxe and flung it over his shoulder like a small child.

"Ready to dig?" he asked the others.

"I guess," Tom responded. He shook his head. John's voice boomed in the rafters; dust fell onto their faces. He didn't like John and he didn't like working in the mines. "Come on, Jer. I think we're assigned over there." He pointed toward the opposite direction John took.

Jerry frowned. He knew they were safest when they worked in the veins, but he also knew Jerry had to be comfortable, so he followed his friend to another shaft.

"What gives, Tom? Why we over here?"

"Coal's coal, ain't it?"

"Yeah. I guess."

Axes began swinging, chips of dirt and coal broke loose. "Think we can get one of those coal carts over here?"

"We'd have one if we'd gone with the others."

"Yeah, but we didn't." Tom looked around and found a foreman. "Hey, Mike! Think you can get us a cart? Big vein of coal over here."

"Sure, Tom." Mike looked around, frowning. The carts holding coal all moved to the entrance. "Sorry, Tom. You'll have to wait. They'll be back in about fifteen; I'll get ya one then."

"That's okay. Thanks, Mike. Just don't forget us over here."

"Won't do that. Just keep digging."

Tom and Jerry looked around. The coal deposits in the shaft were large. If they kept digging now, they'd have to stop and pick up the coal later. Instead, they chipped around the ground; Mike didn't watch Jerry. He knew the man had the resolve of an ox and wouldn't waste time.

"We need to be digging around the coal, at least. That way, when the cart gets back here, we can just loosen it up the rest and drop it into the cart."

"Sounds like a plan." They continued digging for a while before Tom's curiosity got the best of him. "So, tell me more about that big guy."

"Well, I heard he used to live in New Orleans. Think he had a fight with a guy, or something. Killed the guy over a woman."

"No kidding! What's he doing here? He doesn't sound stable."

"I don't think it was like that, Tom. He's here because he's free, ain't he? Must be more to the story than what I heard. Hell, who knows if it's true? Folks talk, you know?"

"Yeah. I know." Tom struck at a loose bit of dirt and a heavy chunk of coal fell to the ground. "Shit!" It fell and rolled dangerously close to landing on his foot. "Good thing we wear these steel-toe jobs."

The rest of the day was uneventful, or, it should have been. Fifteen minutes before shift change, a tired miner walking back to the staging area dropped his pickaxe. He tried to catch it before it hit the ground but missed; it bounced dangerously toward a main load-bearing timber.

"Shit! That was close!" he grumbled, looking around to see if anyone saw his mistake. One poorly planted axe and a beam would come down, taking the miners with it.

"Gage, what're you thinking? Don't do shit like that!" He didn't get away with his error; Mike, the foreman, saw him nearly take out twenty men.

"Sorry, Mike. Guess I'm just tired. Didn't get good sleep last night. Nancy wouldn't stop nagging."

Tom shook his head. He'd avoided the woman and found a good wife instead, but apparently Nancy Pettyjohn got her nails into Gage. "Hey, man, I hear ya!"

"What did you hear?" Gage was in no mood to listen to a coworker disrespect the woman he meant to tame and marry.

"Nothing. Sorry. Didn't realize I'd be hitting such a

sensitive spot. Good luck, is all."

Gage mumbled something and nodded his head before walking toward John. "Hey, John. You up for a beer after we get out?"

"Naw. I got things ta do, man. Maybe 'nother time."

Gage grinned and clasped John on the shoulder, though he had to reach up above his head to do so. "Man, I sure hope to hell you stopped growin'. You won't fit if you don't."

"Think I'm done, Gage." John shook his head. He had heard 'em all his whole life.

The transport cars rolled into the staging area and everyone crawled in, three to a car, John by himself. He liked it that way, never liked to make waves or make himself known. He preferred it that way.

The men dragged their feet; soot and coal dust covered their faces, coated their nostrils and tear ducts. Old pickup trucks and cars on their last hope rolled from the parking lot to homes not much better than the vehicles that carried the men there.

"Tom, what are you fussin' about? I can't imagine you having that hard a time. Get yourself into the shower and wash that shit off your body before you try to kiss me." Mary pushed him away and wiped her hands together before washing them in the kitchen sink. "I have dinner near ready. You'll have to hurry."

"Okay, okay." He continued reminding himself he'd done better with Mary than with Nancy, but it was hard on days when his exhaustion clashed with her boredom.

Tom looked around the pristine home. Black marks marred the clean carpet at the front door. He shook his head, feeling guilty he'd done that to his wife's hard work. "I'm sorry, Mary. I'll be happy when I've washed this grime off."

"You better. We're having company. I want you on your best behavior."

"Company? Mary," Tom whined. The last thing he wanted was to sit around talking to people. He had an early morning at the mine and didn't want to lose precious, needed sleep.

"It's no big deal, Tom. Just some guys from the mines. I thought I'd feed 'em a home-cooked meal."

"Oh. I guess that's alright, then. Who's coming?"

"I invited Jerry and Gage…"

"And?" Tom knew Mary well enough to know she hesitated to tell him something she feared he wouldn't like.

"John Baker."

"Who's…oh. No, Mary," he whined again. "Not that monster. He'll eat us outta house and home."

"Now, you just stop that, Tom Mitchel. You don't know that one bit. He's been in town a while but hasn't a friend I know of. Everyone avoids him…"

Tom interrupted. "No kidding! He's a beast, Mary. Everyone's afraid of him."

"That's just not true. I'm not afraid of him."

"You outta be."

"Go on. Get in that shower and stop messing up my clean floor!"

Tom ducked his head in time for a dish towel to fly over.

Dinner was pleasant; chicken, mashed potatoes, fresh green beans cooked on the stovetop with bacon and green onions, and homemade biscuits fed the group with little effort. Mary laughed and joked with the men; Tom tried, but stared, too often, at John.

John sat politely at the end of the table and took moderate amounts of everything. Tom noticed but didn't say anything. "Eat up, John. If you're hungry, eat. There's more in the kitchen."

"That's alright, Mrs. Mitchel. I've got enough here."

Tom shook his head. He wondered if John truly only ate what he took or if he tried being polite. Either way, John almost endeared himself to his host--almost.

When everyone ate their fill, the men thanked Mary. Jerry and Mike kissed her on the cheek, John nodded but kept his distance.

"Well, we best be going. Daylight comes early and I want you all wide awake. Mary," Mike nodded, and everyone left.

"John, you need a ride?" Jerry looked around; he only saw three cars, his, Mike's and Tom's.

"Naw. I got legs, can walk."

"Suit yourself. Don't say I didn't ask."

"Huh?"

"Never mind, John. Be careful; night's fallin' fast these days."

"Okay. Bye."

The men all made their way home; John walked to a motel in town and took the stairs to his room. He tugged his shirt off, kicked his boots to the corner and dropped, exhausted, onto his bed.

It complained, creaking beneath his girth, even though the motel had reinforced the bed in his room to accommodate his bulk.

Morning always comes too early. This day was no different than the hundreds before. Tom rolled out of bed after briefly hugging Mary's pillow. She arose an hour before him to make breakfast and lunch and start her own day.

"Good morning, sleepyhead."

Tom stumbled into the kitchen, scratching beneath his boxers. He leaned forward and kissed Mary on the cheek. "What's that amazing smell?"

"Just some pork chops for your sandwiches today."

"Doesn't smell like pork chops."

"I'm cooking some peppers and onions to go on them. I thought you'd like something a little different."

"What's the occasion?"

"You. I wanted to thank you."

"For?"

"For being such a good host last night. You were so polite."

"Uh…"

"I mean, you didn't let John put you off. You talked and laughed and treated our guests really nice."

"Okay. If you say so." Tom walked away from the stove to sit at the table. He scratched his head, wondering why his wife would think he wouldn't be nice to people she'd invited into their home.

He finished eating a hearty breakfast and grabbed his hardhat and jacket. As Tom walked toward the door, Mary handed him the lunchbox.

"Don't forget this. You'll starve without it."

"Thanks, Mary. Always looking out for me."

"Of course. Don't want to lose you to something like an empty stomach!"

"Never happen."

Tom left after kissing Mary. "Another day of dirt and grime. Hooray!"

The mine stood open, as always. The gaping hole at the entrance always made Tom think of a huge beast waiting to chew and digest those who so willingly enter its mouth.

"Hey, Tom. You thank your wife for dinner. Haven't eaten like that for…I don't even know how long." Mike patted Tom on the back.

"You didn't thank her?"

"Of course I did, but it was so good, it's worth mentioning twice."

Jerry interrupted the others. "You invited John to your house? That was right nice of you."

"Didn't do anything like that. All Mary, there."

Jerry frowned. He wondered what Tom had against John. He knew the man hadn't spoken to him much the night before but thought it was because he was tired like the rest of them.

"Let's get a front car so we can take the same shaft we had yesterday."

Jerry nodded but kept quiet. His mind kept returning to Tom and how he treated, or didn't treat, John.

They reached the mile mark underground again, and everyone poured from their cars. John stayed behind, watching where each miner walked. He took a shaft of his own and began his day.

John enjoyed working in the mines. He didn't have to talk to others, and nobody bothered him. He flung the axe like he was born to it. By himself, he dug as much coal as five men.

Every miner worked hard every day, dirt and coal dust seeped into their noses, eyes, clothes, and even skin. Most had long ago ceased complaints. It did no good; everyone did what they did to pay their bills and feed their families.

Break time came and went. Tom shared his massive lunch with Jerry who had a bologna sandwich and a small bag of chips. "Look over there."

Tom looked where Jerry pointed. John sat against the wall, his eyes closed, his log-like arms and legs crossed in front of him. He snored lightly.

"Think he's got some food?"

"Don't know. Not my problem. Not yours either."

Jerry stood. "Be right back."

"Jer…"

Jerry approached John and stood quietly to his side. "Hey, John."

John opened an eye. "Yeah?"

"Hungry?"

"Nope." His stomach rumbled after the lie left his lips. "Guess, maybe a little."

"Here. I got plenty." Jerry gave his sandwich and chips to John. "Sorry it's not much."

"I can't eat your lunch. You need it."

"Don't think about it. I ate plenty, already. Take this. Can't work like you do and not need food."

"Thanks." John took the food and wolfed it down like he'd not eaten for a week.

Jerry returned to Tom. Gage stopped him on the way. "You did a good thing."

Jerry looked at Gage. "Thanks."

Break ended and everyone returned to work.

Gage followed John. "You need some help?"

"Nope."

"You sure? Awful lonely digging by yourself."

"I'm good."

Gage frowned. He only wanted to make friends with the big man. "Okay. Holler if you want to talk to someone."

"Okay. Thanks."

From the Diaphragm

Axes clanged against stone and dirt. The rhythm many of the miners created nearly sounded melodious. They enjoyed when their work became more than just metal to rock.

Gage returned to the shaft he'd worked that morning. He tripped on several rocks fallen to the ground. "Jesus! Gotta kick that shit away, so nobody gets hurt!"

"Sorry, man. Kick 'em away if you want 'em moved," one of the miners told Gage.

"Guess I'll have to. You can just call me 'mom'."

"Mom shut your mouth and get to work," Mike came up behind the man.

"Yeah, okay."

Work continued.

"Shush! What's that sound?"

Miners closest to the sound stopped digging. They craned their necks to direct their ears toward the unknown sound.

Further away, more men noticed others not digging and they complained.

"Shut up!"

Finally, the entire shaft silenced like a grave. A slight noise, not more than a whisper; something crackled behind them.

"Is that a beam cracking?"

"Naw. Can't be. Those beams are tested before they're put down here, ain't they?"

"S'posed to be."

"I know they came from the miller down the road."

"Chris always does us right."

"Yeah."

"What are you guys doing? There's nothing being done!"

"Sorry, Mike. Thought we heard something."

Just then, a loud crack startled the group. Tom and Jerry ran to the shaft. "Hey, what's that noise?"

Everyone looked at the timbers around them. "Nothing here. Maybe it's just dirt falling."

Crack!

Dust began spewing into the shaft the men dug. They started hearing rock and timbers falling, splintering and landing on the ground.

The men began to scramble around; panic fed each man differently. Tom sat in the corner, hugged his knees, and quietly prayed he would live through the day. Jerry and Mike tried to keep everyone calm and find an escape route.

Gage and others felt their hearts beating through their chests, their throats clogging with tears and dust.

They began to make peace with themselves. They spent several minutes praying for God's forgiveness or shouting to the timbers that still stood.

When all felt they'd lose their lives, a shadow emerged through the dust and falling timbers. A big man, larger than any other, stood near a falling timber. He grabbed it and shoved it up, making room for the rest of the men to escape.

"Go! I got this!" John's veins strained against his skin. Sweat glistened, pouring so much his shirt and jeans clung to his body. He shoved against the timber; one of the men shouted. "I can see light up there!" They scrambled to follow the light.

Outside, miners, wives and coworkers stood by; they worried for the men in the mines. Dust spewed from the mouth, telling them little hope remained for the men inside.

From the hole John created, men began to climb into the fresh air.

"Someone's still in there! We gotta get him! He saved us all!"

Men grabbed jacks, timbers, and tools before heading back into the mine. A few feet in, the ground began to rumble. The earth cracked and spat forth gas and smoke. The men ran from the mine, once more, angry with themselves for being too afraid to help the one man who gave his own life so they could live.

Tom started taking a collection. "We have to mark this mine."

"Come on, Tom. Don't you think it's enough that we lost a man down there?" Jerry looked from Tom to Mike. "We ain't going back down there, Mike."

"Don't think it's possible, Jerry. Too dangerous. Plenty more mines built better."

Tom frowned. "Come on, guys. Pony up. Gotta do something for Big John. He saved us all!"

Jerry had misread Tom's intentions and started walking with Tom. "Give what you can. John saved your life." He kept up with Tom. "Hey. What are you thinking?"

"Thought we'd mark the man's grave with a stone."

Jerry liked that idea very much. "What are you gonna put on it?"

"At the bottom of this mine lies a big, big man, Big John."

Sweet Molly Malone

Dublin, what a timeless city. I walk the streets, watching the hustle and bustle of the day.

Today, I took a different route; I stepped off the path where most of the rich, fancy, employed, capable people walked and ventured into an alley.

A wheelbarrow rested, crooked on a loose wheel, at the back of the alley. A young girl, not more than nine or ten, stood beside it. She called out to any who walked by.

"Sir, would you buy from me? I have mollusks and mussels for sale."

Not fond of shellfish, I turned down her offer. It would seem I broke the girl's heart; she looked so forlorn. "That is alright, sir. At least you did not walk by and ignore me like the others."

Her sweet little voice, her humility, and the briefest of tales from her light-pink lips tore my heart from my chest as though impaled with a hundred jagged-edged daggers.

"Well, perhaps I can help you in another way?" I offered and approached the girl.

She shuddered, squeaked, and ran behind her decrepit cart. "Oh, no, sir. That is alright. I manage well, enough."

I stopped walking. I had no intention of scaring the child. I merely thought to assist her in tightening the bolt holding the barrow's wheel in place. "I mean you no harm, child. My name is Seamus. What is yours?"

"I am Molly, if it please you, sir."

"It pleases me very well. You are a strong one, like my very own mum."

"Your mum?"

"Aye. Her name is Molly, too!"

"Oh!" Her blue eyes lit up, even in the shadows of the foreboding alley. "That is so nice."

"Thank you. Would you allow me to take a few minutes to fix your wheel? It looks hard to push that way."

She looked shyly at her fingers, afraid to allow me near. My father warns me of dangerous, strange men."

I was strange, to be sure—to her. "No worries, Molly. If you like, I will stand out here on the busy street until you come here, and I will then go fix your wheel while you enjoy the heat." I held my breath, somehow praying she would agree to my terms.

She hopped from one foot to the other. Her clothes, torn and tattered, barely reached her knees. She wore no stockings and one shoe had a hole at the toe. The poor child must be freezing in that corner. "Come on, Molly. I vow I will not hurt you."

Finally, Molly decided to trust me. I stood far from her wheelbarrow, in the middle of the walkway. When she came close enough, I moved to the side of the alley furthest from her trek. "Alright. You stand here in the sun and warm your fingers and toes. I will go look to your wheelbarrow."

She nodded and held onto a pole wielding a vendor's shingle.

It took me less than ten minutes to tighten the bolt. I clapped my hands together and walked to Molly. "There you go, child. You can now push your cart and reach more people who would buy your goods."

"They are very good, sir!" she exclaimed before running to her shellfish.

"Molly, if I may?"

"What do you need?"

"I would ask you; why are you pushing a wheelbarrow with a broken wheel down the streets of Dublin? Where are your mum and da?"

"My mum is dead; God rest her soul. My da throws his net at the shore. He catches this and I sell it to the people. The wheel went lame this morn' and I was stuck where I stood, trying to sell these."

She pushed the wheelbarrow past me and into the sunshine. "You should take care to keep to the shadows. The sun may spoil your wares before you can sell them."

She looked up into the rare sunshine and smiled. "Thank you, sir."

I went along my way, praying the motherless child would not find herself working the entire day to sell the mussels and mollusks. That was much too big a job for such a small child.

The next day, I found myself traveling the same walk

at the same time of day. I thought to give the girl some money or a warm meal. After all, we introduced ourselves and I did her a favor, so no longer can we be called strangers.

Molly struggled, this day. The wheelbarrow appeared heavier than the day before. I felt sorely saddened to watch the child fight with it.

"Molly! Would you allow me to help you?"

"No, sir! That would be inappropriate. We are strangers and you have no responsibility to me."

"Your da has responsibility to you, but where is he?"

"He is working hard at the piers. He wants to catch fish and shrimp, mussels and mollusks for me to sell."

"And why would he not catch in the morning and sell by himself in the evening while people walk to their homes?"

"I would never ask him to help me. It is my duty to sell that which he nets and brings to shore."

I shrugged. "Would you allow me to buy you lunch, at least?"

The girl shook her head. "No, sir. That would not be appropriate, either."

"I wondered how a child so young would know such words, but I assume a difficult life comes with education before one's time."

"Very well. I bid you farewell, young Molly. Godspeed to you."

Molly smiled and pushed the cart, sneezing twice before she left my side. I could hear her singing a lovely tune and felt her talents wasted in the brutal, wet, late-autumn rain but she refused my offers, twice.

"Seamus, where have you been? School let out two hours past."

"I know, Mum. I merely walked the streets, enjoying the weather."

My mother frowned and chuckled. "This weather has nothing to be enjoyed, does it?" She heard the rain spattering against the clay tiles on our roof.

I put my book bag on the table and kissed her cheek. "There is a wee bit of rain."

"Wee bit? Torrents are less than this."

I knew she spoke truth, but I had to go see the girl downtown. I had to know she was alright. "Alright, Mum. I will tell you. I went to town and walked the streets looking for a girl."

"Girl! You are barely sixteen! What girl would you need to seek?"

"Och, not like that, Mum. This is a child. A wee thing not more than eight years. I saw her yesterday and again today. I fixed her wheelbarrow wheel yesterday. It wobbled and she could not push it."

"A wee girl pushing a wheelbarrow? Why?"

"Her da has her push it to sell shellfish." I felt my nose wrinkle up in distaste, not of the shellfish which I despise, but for a little girl being forced to work so hard when she should be in school."

"That is so sad. Why was she not in school?"

"I did not ask, but Mum, you should hear her sing!

Like an angel, she sounds."

"Sounds like you may have some feeling for the child. You are her age twice over!"

"I am not in love with her, Mum!" I shook my head in disbelief. I suppose my mum was interested in me growing up and giving her grandbabies, but I would not until I finished uni.

"I should hope not!" Mum winked at me.

I spent the evening as I did every evening, nose in books, thoughts on other things. Tonight, though, my thoughts were on the little girl in the big city, pushing a wheelbarrow around, hawking shellfish.

Sleep did not come; my mind whirling with the thoughts of maths, science, biology, and…Molly.

"Dearling, did you not sleep at all?" My mum asked when I tripped down the stairs to greet her for breakfast. "School is getting too difficult?"

"No, Mum. Well, no, I did not sleep well, though I slept. Too many thoughts in my head."

"Too many? What thoughts would keep a healthy young lad from sleeping restfully?"

"School." I didn't expand on that. She nodded in understanding.

"Well, eat up, Seamus. Food will give you energy to greet your day."

"It is Saturday. No school, today."

Mum opened her mouth to speak more but I interrupted her.

"I thought I would go into town and see if I can find

a job."

"A job. Why would you want a job? School is your job. Your exams are your job. A future at uni is your job."

"I know, but I have something I want to buy."

"What is it, love? I will get it for you."

"Nothing. Frivolity is all. Something I do not need; just want it."

Mum seemed satisfied with my answer and returned to frying sausages and tomatoes for my breakfast.

I nearly choked on my food, wolfing it down to get through it and out the door.

"Do not forget your mack. It is supposed to rain."

I grabbed a raincoat from the hook by the door and ran through it, still chewing a bite of toast. "Bye, Mum. Be back by dinner."

"Be careful."

I rode my motorbike to Dublin; thankful the sky did not open and pour water over me. I rode slowly through the busy streets. The city seemed to argue against my forward progress.

There, standing under an awning, arguing with a shopkeeper, Molly stood, shivering. Her damaged shoe looking worse than just two days before. The entire top of the shoe gone, her toes peeking out, a strange blue hue at the tips.

"She is freezing! Can you not see that? Let her warm herself in your shop for the love of God!" I shouted as I parked my motorbike at the curb.

"How is this your business?"

"She is a person. A young girl, and you want to treat her like a rat in the streets! That is how this is my business! You are a horrid man!"

Molly stared at me. She looked worse than the day before, too. Her eyes were bloodshot from crying, her nose red and running, but there was more. She looked quite ill.

"Molly, love. Are you alright?"

"I am alright, Seamus. Thank you for what you said."

"What? Anyone with a heart would have done the same."

"No, sir, they would not. No fewer than seven people walked by without saying a word to defend me."

I felt sick to my stomach. How could people be so cruel? This wee child was beautiful, sweet, and hard-working. Why would none come to her aid? "Come with me. I have to do something. I would enjoy your company on my way."

I had five quid in my pocket and a few shillings, besides. That should get a pair of shoes for little feet and perhaps a bit of pastry.

She frowned and glanced at her wheelbarrow. I grabbed the handles. "Come on if you want this back," I teased.

Molly giggled and followed behind, struggling to keep up with her broken shoe, so I slowed my pace.

"Where are we going?"

"I am going to buy you a gift." She opened her mouth to object, but I waved my hand. "You cannot say 'no'. I will not allow it. You will accept this gift."

She clamped her mouth shut, but I noticed her eyes wavering toward a vendor selling pastries and large, bready pretzels. "Would you like one?"

"Oh, I could not ask."

"You have not asked; I offered."

She agreed with my logic and nodded. "I do like the ones with the red inside."

I grinned; I won the battle with no bloodshed.

When we finished with pastries and milk, I took her to a small shop.

"What are we doing here?"

"You need new shoes. I will buy you some."

"How do you have all this money? Are you rich?"

"No, I am not rich. I am just happy to share what I have with a worthy young girl."

She blushed. "You are so kind to me. Why?"

"You deserve it, Molly."

A series of sneezes followed by the worst cough I heard in my lifetime came from this tiny child. They seemed to go on, forever.

"Are you okay?"

She nodded through coughing. I patted her back and glared at many people who walked by and frowned, crossed the street, or otherwise avoided Molly and me.

We entered when she collected herself and stopped

sneezing. "I am so sorry! Perhaps we should not go in. I may make others sick."

I put my hand on her shoulder to guide her into the doorway. "Nonsense." I frowned; even through her clothes, I could feel the burning fever that caused her so much discomfort. "What do you usually eat? You sure did eat up that pastry quickly!"

She giggled. "I do not get sweets often. Thank you." She did not answer my question and I did not press.

"You are welcome."

"May I help you, sir and, err, miss?"

"We need a pair of shoes. I do not know the size. She needs something better to wear. Stockings, too, if they are not too costly."

"You are in luck, young man. If you purchase a pair of shoes, you get a full package of six pairs of stockings."

I looked at the woman in shock. I knew of no sale nor special purchase bargain. When she glanced my way, I saw a sparkle in her eye. She was one of the good ones.

"Thank you, mistress!"

Molly stood stoic and silent at my side after the good news.

We found a suitable pair of ankle boots. They fit perfectly, sturdy, leather shoes with a good, solid sole that would last.

"Can I get any stockings I like?" She finally spoke after sitting quietly to be fitted with a pair of boots.

"Of course, dearling."

Molly hopped from the chair and tripped on the boots. "Oh! I am sorry!" She sat again, embarrassed to be so clumsy.

"Nonsense!" The shopkeeper walked to a display of children's stockings. "Why do I not bring you several packages to choose from?"

"That would be nice. Thank you."

It was clear the little mollusk vendor was taught properly how to talk with others. I smiled.

After choosing a pack of thick, practical, and pink stockings, the boots were upsized one to suit the thickness, and the purchase rung up. I paid two shillings for the pastries, two more for milk, and two pounds for a pair of shoes and six pair of stockings.

When I looked at the receipt after paying, I saw I received a seventy-percent discount on the shoes. I grinned at the woman who nodded toward Molly. "I could not. I just could not say no."

We left and said our goodbyes to each other before I returned to my motorbike near the rude shopkeeper's door and drove home. I could not think of a better use of my day and my money.

"You are home early."

"Nobody is hiring teenagers now, Mum. I suppose school will be my job a bit longer."

I did not fool my mum, not even a little. "Mm hmm."

Saturday was spent mowing, cleaning, dusting,

digging, and reading in the evening. I helped my da with his chores to speed them to completion.

We ate dinner at the table as we did every Saturday. The weekdays, too hectic, found us eating when we could, what we could. Saturday and Sunday were family dinners and Sunday church.

"How was your day, son?"

I looked at my father. He did not speak often, but when he did, I knew better than ignore. "It was…productive."

Da laughed. He thought I meant all the work we had done. "I know that, but you were not here all morning. Where did you go?"

"It seems our Seamus has a wee friend in town."

Yes, I knew I had not fooled my mum.

"Oh?"

"Not like that, Da. She is a wee child. Her shoes were so broken one fell from her foot. She is starving and I fear she is ill."

"Ill? Oh no! Why do you think that?" Mum was always looking for a poor soul to help. I guess that is where I got it.

"I helped her through the shopkeeper's door and could feel fever through her coat. She also broke into a fit of sneezes and coughing. Her coughs sounded like those of the old men who smoke too much."

"She does not smoke, right?"

"Da, she's eight!"

Da nodded and continued eating.

"I would like to bring her to church tomorrow, if I can find her and her da will allow it."

"That would be nice, son." Da understood Mum's need to help others and that I thought the same.

I grinned and finished dinner with a new appreciation for my family. "Thank you. I will go in the morning and seek her out."

The rest of the evening, uneventful, became a time to catch up on lost sleep. My mind did not spin with concern over the child this night.

Morning broke and I awoke before the sun cleared the horizon. I quickly dressed and grabbed an apple before driving to the city streets in search of my little friend.

"Have you seen Molly?"

"Who?"

"Wee girl, pushes a wheelbarrow full of mussels and mollusks."

"Och, I am sorry to tell you, the child collapsed on the street yesterday."

"Collapsed? I saw her just yesterday morning. She appeared ill, but nothing so bad."

"A woman rushed from that shop and tried to revive the girl, but she would not awaken."

I felt that same sick feeling in my stomach. Did my friend die? Was she in the hospital? Did her da know where she lay? "Where is she?"

"The ambulance took her away. I do not know where she is."

I returned home and collected my family.

"Where is the child? Could you not find her?"

"She is ill, Mum. I do not know where she is. A woman said she collapsed yesterday, and nobody knows where the ambulance took her."

Mum reached over and patted my hand. "We will ask the minister to pray for her."

"That would be good, I think. She needs our prayers."

Church went as expected. Sing some songs, listen to the word of God as interpreted by our geriatric minister, and then calls for prayers. I stood and asked for the congregation to pray for little Molly. "I am sorry, I do not know her full name. We only just met three days past. She pushes a wheelbarrow along the streets of downtown Dublin, selling mollusks and mussels."

"I know the lass," an old man three pews away spoke. "Her da speaks to me when we throw our nets. Malone. Her name is Molly Malone. I did not see her da this morning. I wonder if he has found his girl."

"His girl did not make it through the night." A nurse across from me spoke. "I know the girl. Wee thing with black hair and bright, blue eyes."

"That is her." I choked back a sob. My friend died alone of a fever I should have reported. "This is my fault! I should have told someone! I should have taken her somewhere!"

The minister spoke then. "She is with God, Seamus. Do not think yourself at fault. God takes those he finds worthy. Your friend, Molly Malone, is with God. He holds her tight to his side and keeps her safe in Heaven."

The words did not soothe my guilt, but I nodded in thanks.

Services ended and we stood with the others to leave. When I reached to shake the minister's hand, beside him stood a small child with dark hair and bright-blue eyes. Molly stood, clean and smiling, beside him. "What…?"

The minister took my hand and shook it. "You have a good heart, Seamus. You are a good man."

I glanced at the minister but returned to look at his side.

"I am alright, Seamus." I heard the child's voice plain.

"You're here! I thought you dead! The nurse…"

"She is right, Seamus. I passed in the night. Now, I will walk by your side to keep you safe."

I shuddered. Would I be haunted all my days by a restless spirit? Even Molly, who would not harm a soul, would be a disconcerting companion through time.

I sat in the back, Da drove, and we returned home. My body took its own course to the garden behind the house. Cabbage, potatoes, and beans sat neatly between a variety of more colorful fare. I sat on a bench and kicked loose chunks of dirt.

"Do not mourn my loss, Seamus. You showed me kindness I did not deserve." Molly sat beside me, holding my hand in her ghostly shadows.

"You…I just…why?"

"God told me my suffering should end. He waited, you know, until you cared for me as you could. Thank you, by the way, for the beautiful stockings and the pastry. You are going to be a good man. God told me you are not yet one."

I smirked through the tears that threatened. "Not yet, no."

"You do not need to worry, Seamus. God has great plans for you."

"Do you intend to follow me through life?" A question I pondered.

"No. I am here to help you through this loss you seem to feel you have. I will see my da, then I will leave to my place among the children God has rescued from their own sorrows."

I shook my head, closed my eyed, and took a deep breath. "I shall miss you, Molly."

"We will meet again."

Then, she stood, took the handles of a filled wheelbarrow, and rolled away, fading into the relentless mist that accompanied the weather. I felt oddly relieved; my spirit cleaned of any guilt and sorrow. Molly would never suffer again.

The Way

"You have the toothpaste?"

"I do. I also packed soap, your special towels, your sexy underwear, and your c-pap machine. We're ready to go if you are."

"I was born ready!"

Terry and Sandy giggled and laughed as they prepared for their trip across the country. Neither had a specific destination, agreeing the journey had a better chance of success without one.

"Here, you carry this; it is so heavy!" Sandy asked Terry.

"What? I packed pretty much everything!" Terry looked at Sandy's pout and shrugged. "Oh, alright. You know how much I can't resist those puppy dog eyes."

Sandy rolled the larger luggage to the car's trunk. "I brought this one, but could you help me lift it into the car?"

Terry smiled and leaned over to hook his hand under the bottom of the suitcase and lifted it with Sandy's help into the deep chasm of a trunk of their Passat.

"Whew! I'm so glad we bought this car. The trunk is so roomy!"

Terry smiled. "Come on. Let's double-check the house and lock up. I bet we'll be gone a while."

"Alright!" Sandy skipped to the house and turned

around before opening the door. "Maybe you should go remind the neighbors we're leaving so they know to check our mail and get the papers off the porch."

"Good idea. You're always thinking!" Terry turned to the left and approached the big, white house on the corner. He knocked on the door and a portly woman answered.

"Terry, what a wonderful surprise! I thought you and Sandy already left!"

"Not yet, but just about, Mrs. Brooks. We're going in a few minutes. Just wanted to be sure you knew we left. So, you're still okay with checking our mail and house?"

"Of course, dear. Oh! Wait here. I have a little gift for you two."

Terry and Sandy loved Mrs. Brooks' oatmeal raisin cookies. He hoped that would be her gift to them.

As hoped, Mrs. Brooks returned to the door with a tin of cookies. "I baked you some cookies for the trip."

She leaned to the right of the door and grabbed an insulated bag. "Something to drink."

Terry looked confused. The woman seemed anxious for them to leave, but when he opened the bag and saw two large bottles of wine, he grinned. "You know us so well!"

"You have a safe trip. Send lots of post cards! Don't drink that while you're still driving." Mrs. Brooks leaned forward and hugged Terry. "Tell Sandy I want him over here so I can send him off with my love, too."

"I will, Mrs. Brooks. Thanks so much for the lovely gifts! We will enjoy them."

"I do hope so." Mrs. Brooks waved Terry away from the door and closed it. Before it closed completely, Terry heard her sniffle.

"Aww, don't cry."

She giggled before the latch clicked.

He looked toward his house. The door remained open. "Sandy, goodness, there'll be flies inside," he muttered to himself. "Oh well, they'll die soon enough without anything to eat."

Just as he passed the sidewalk that led to their door, Sandy came out. "Alright! I turned off the breakers and checked the stove; gas is all shut off. Anything else?"

"Windows? Back door?"

"Yep. I have that letter we wrote, too." Sandy patted his pocket.

"Good. Glad you thought of it. Oh, Mrs. Brooks says come by. She wants to tell you goodbye before we drive off."

"Oh, I love Mrs. Brooks! Did she…Oh! She gave us cookies, didn't she?"

"She did, and wine!"

Sandy giggled and clapped his fingers against his palm. "I'll go right now…if it's okay."

"Go on. I've got this. You did your part; I'm going to finish mine."

Sandy skipped to Mrs. Brooks' front door. Before he had a chance to knock, the door flew open and the woman grabbed Sandy. "I will miss our sewing circles, Sandy. You do such lovely embroidery!"

"I'll do more on the road and send it to you, honey, promise." Sandy gave Mrs. Brooks a peck on the cheek and stood back from her. "Thank you for the wine and cookies. I will totally enjoy them!"

The woman sniffled and wiped her eyes with her apron. "You are so kind to say."

"I don't just say. We love your cookies."

"Here are some other snacks. You can't live on cookies all by themselves."

Sandy took a huge Styrofoam box from Mrs. Brooks. "Go on, look inside."

He smiled at her. "Oh! Grapes and blueberries, sandwiches and sliced zucchini and yellow squash! What a lovely gift, Mrs. Brooks. You spoil us."

"I love spoiling my favorite boys."

Sandy gave Mrs. Brooks another hug before skipping to the car. He opened the back door and carefully put the gift on the seat. He stacked other items around it to keep it from tilting and spilling.

"What's that?" Terry asked, nodding at the cooler.

"Mrs. Brooks gave us some munchies and sandwiches."

"She spoils us."

"That, she does."

"Ready?"

"Ooh, yes. I'm so ready!"

Terry sat behind the steering wheel and started the

car. "Buckle up, buttercup. We're off to the great beyond."

"The final frontier." Sandy giggled.

"That's space, goofy."

"Which way?"

Terry shrugged. "Point."

Sandy closed his eyes and flung his hand around his head, stopping his finger pointing toward the east. "Perfect! That's the long way!"

"Bye-bye, California!" They left their San Diego home and drove east along Interstate-8 toward destinations unknown.

"I'm so glad we decided to do this instead of just wasting time, slacking at the pool and only getting sunburnt and then tanned."

"I do love your swarthy skin, Terry. You look so lovely with a tan. But, I do agree, this is amazing. We have the money and we have the time. Let's just keep on going."

"Eastward bound."

On the border of Arizona, the couple stopped for a snack. "We stopping in Cali or Arizona?"

"We should leave California, I think." Terry looked over to Sandy to check for approval. He found his partner thoughtful. "Look, a rest area. We can stop there and sit in the shade at a picnic table."

"Wonderful!" Sandy grabbed the cooler, and Terry the bag of wine and tin of cookies. "I thought we could save the cookies to munch on while we drive."

Terry looked at the tin then Sandy. He shrugged. "Alright. That's a good idea." The tin returned to the back seat.

Sandy nodded. "There's fruit and stuff in here. That's enough sweets while we eat lunch."

"Oh!" Terry realized he didn't know if they had any cups to drink the wine.

"What is it? Is something wrong?"

"No. Well, not really. It's just we don't have anything to drink the wine with."

"Of course we do. Didn't you see?"

Sandy reached into the wine bag and tugged a bottle out. Cupped at the bottom, two plastic tumblers.

"Mrs. Brooks truly spoils us."

Sandy grinned and nodded. A tuft of white-blond hair fell over his eyes. He blew it away and giggled. "No worries on this trip, right?"

Terry reached over and combed Sandy's hair back with his fingers. "No worries at all."

They sat away from others, unsure the response of the population of travelers. They didn't like to make waves.

"So, Mrs. Brooks will check our mail and Mr. Jenkins said he'd mow our yard."

"That is so nice of them. We have the best neighbors ever."

"We do."

Terry and Sandy relaxed in the breeze blowing beneath the concrete cover over their resting place. One bottle of wine gone, the two remained lost in each other, talking about everything and nothing at all. They spoke of their hopes to see every inch of the country and how they would get along together for the rest of their lives. "And beyond," Sandy agreed.

The two finished lunch and got back in the car. "Shall we?"

"We shall."

They drove into Arizona and across the Rocky Mountains. "This is beautiful! Look at all those trees!" Sandy wiggled in his seat like a child, excited to see things he'd never seen before on the coast of California.

"It is. I remember my mom and dad bringing us here in the summer. Maybe we can find Estes Park. That's a skiing resort."

"That's neat! I'd like to go skiing one day."

"Maybe we can do it when winter comes. That's an awful long wait, though, seeing it is May."

Sandy giggled, agreeing with his partner. "How about we turn north, now?"

"North it is. Look at the map; what is the next main interstate?"

"Why do we want to take interstates? How about we take the unbeaten path? Let's be adventurous!"

Terry didn't like the idea of breaking away from main highways, but he couldn't tell Sandy no. "Alright. Find a road you like, and we'll take it. Has to be to the left, now, or we'll end up in Mexico."

Sandy took Terry's advice seriously. He stared at the road and watched carefully, always keeping his eye to the left of the car. "There! Up ahead. Let's take that one."

Terry looked at the path Sandy chose. It looked destitute and maybe even private. "You're sure."

"Positive. That one. It said 'take me! Take me!'."

"I'll take you!" Terry teased. "Any day. I'll take you any day!"

"Aww." Sandy looked lovingly toward Terry.

They drove for hours down the wooded half-dirt, half-asphalt road.

Back in San Diego, Terry and Sandy's adopted son, Troy, called his parents. Nobody answered the phone, which worried Troy. "They always answer. Something's wrong."

Troy's wife hugged him to calm his worry. "Maybe they went to the store?"

"It's not Tuesday. They always go to the store on Tuesday. Creatures of habit, my dads."

"That much, huh?"

"Uh huh. Laundry is Saturday morning, groceries Tuesdays, church Sunday. They cook for the week on Wednesday and Thursday and do cleaning every morning at seven. Total OCD duo."

"Well, it's good to have schedules, isn't it?"

"Yes, dear. It is good to have schedules. Daddy T taught me that when I was young."

"Then, don't worry. Maybe they're changing things up a little. Maybe they overslept or are in the shower. Maybe Terry is mowing the lawn or Sandy is gardening."

"I guess you're right. I wish they'd get a cell phone. I can't reach them when they're not at home or in the house."

"I know, honey. Don't worry. Let's just drive over and see if they're outside."

Troy agreed with Teresa, his wife. They left their downtown townhouse loft and drove to the suburb home where Troy grew up.

"Where's the car?" Troy asked. "The car should be here!" He peered into the garage; nobody seemed to be home.

"Hello! Hello? Oh, Troy! It's you and your pretty wife." Mrs. Brooks rushed to the garage.

"Hi, Mrs. Brooks. I hate to bother you, but have you seen my dads?"

"Of course, I have. They left early this morning."

"Left? They never go anywhere. Where could they have gone?"

"Oh dear. They didn't talk to you? They decided to take a road trip. Kind of a 'Route-66' trip. They didn't even know where they would visit."

"That doesn't sound like my dads. You sure they didn't give you an itinerary and a way to contact them?"

"Not even a direction, I'm afraid, Troy."

Troy stood quietly, breathing steadily to keep his nerves from exploding and forcing him to do or say something he knew he would regret. He silently thanked his parents for teaching him how to control his temper. "Nothing? Well, that is odd."

"I don't see why that would be odd," Mrs. Brooks replied.

"They are really habitual. They like schedules and plans. They use lists to shop for…well, for everything. I can't believe they just picked up and left."

"They did. You can ask Mr. Jenkins. Terry talked to both of us this morning."

"I think that isn't necessary. Did they leave you a key, by any chance?"

"You don't have one?"

Tony shook his head. "When I moved out, I left it behind. Not my place, anymore, ya know?"

"That is thoughtful. If you don't have access, you can't be expected to just drop in." Mrs. Brooks frowned. She wished Troy tried harder to stay part of his family. Terry and Sandy were such lovely parents and raised the young man well.

"The key?"

"Oh, of course!" She reached into her pocket and pulled a key on a lanyard from her pocket. "I didn't want to lose it."

"Good thinking." Troy tugged the rainbow lanyard over his head and took his wife by the hand. "Thank you, Mrs. Brooks. We'll go inside and make sure everything is okay, then. Thanks, again."

"Of course, Troy. Don't be a stranger!"

"No, ma'am."

Troy and Teresa entered the house. Nothing looked out of place. Troy flipped the switch, but nothing turned on. "Hmm."

"Maybe they flipped the breakers?"

"That sounds like my dads," Troy agreed.

They flipped a few more switches, proving their hypothesis true.

"Do you think they shut off the gas and water, too?"

"Wouldn't put it past them."

The couple walked through the house. Troy didn't see the luggage under the bed and that proved Mrs. Brooks' account. "I wonder why they'd just leave without saying anything."

"Maybe they didn't want you talking them out of their great adventure." Teresa didn't mince words. She knew Troy spent a lot of time worrying over his aging fathers.

"Smarty pants." Troy and Teresa left the house and made sure to lock the door before returning the key to Mrs. Brooks.

"Did you find what you were looking for?"

"We did. Thank you. I'll come by in a week or so to see if they're back. Please, tell them we stopped by if you see them or hear from them?"

"I will, of course!"

"Thank you, Mrs. Brooks."

Troy and Teresa left feeling a little better that no harm had come to the older men, but Troy still had the feeling something was *off*.

"Where are we, now, Sandy?" Terry hoped Sandy would be able to read the Rand McNally Atlas they'd bought at the convenience store before leaving San Diego.

"Oh, we're really near a little village. Let's stop there. I still need to send this letter."

Terry agreed. "How far?"

Sandy used a digit on his finger to measure then did mental math to determine the distance based on the atlas key.

"Maybe seven miles."

"Alright. On this winding road, I'd say about ten to fifteen minutes away. Good. I gotta pee, too."

Sandy giggled. "You could just stop, silly. There isn't anyone for miles!"

Terry looked around and through the rear-view mirror. "You're right, but it's so *uncivilized!*"

"Let your hair down. We're on vacation!"

Terry shook his head. He loved Sandy but sometimes his carefree attitude made Terry wonder why he did. "I just can't fling it out. What if someone comes by?"

"Stand behind the car or behind a mountain. I don't care. Why do you have to sit there and suffer?"

"I'm not suffering."

Sandy stared at Terry. "Mhh hmm."

The car rolled along the winding, mountainous road. "I'm getting dizzy." Sandy looked out the window to try to keep his bearings. He did not usually travel well, and the wine took its toll on his stomach. It roiled in complaint.

"Do you want me to stop?"

"No, that's alright. But, maybe you could slow down a little on those curves?"

"I can do that—anything for you, my darling."

Sandy smiled sweetly; he loved when Terry called him that.

"Thank you sweetness."

They made it to the small village; it took nearly thirty minutes at the slower pace, but they really had no place else to be.

Sandy jumped out at a gas station. Terry went inside to pay for the gas and go to the bathroom while Sandy looked for a mailbox. He squealed happily when he saw a blue US Mailbox two blocks down the street.

He looked back and didn't see Terry, so he shrugged and skipped to the mailbox.

"Hey, fag! What're you doing in our town? We don't let just anyone in our town."

Sandy ignored the hateful comments. He was not going to let anyone make him upset. Besides, on the scale of insults, the young men's comments were very low, nearly unmeasurable.

"Didn't you hear me, fag? You ain't allowed her."

Sandy muttered beneath his breath, "This is a free country; I have every right to walk down the street."

He looked at his choice of travel clothes and regretted it. Floral blouses and pink jeans were probably not the best choice as they traveled across the country. "I should change before we get further into Arizona."

He rushed quickly to the mailbox, shoved the letter inside, and ran back to the car. He felt a twinge of fear; the young men didn't ignore him. Instead, they started walking in his direction.

"We told ya. Your kind ain't welcome here."

Terry took that moment to leave the gas station and returned to the car. As small as Sandy was, Terry stood twelve inches taller; his body buff and fit from years of working out. "Sandy, get in the car, okay, honey? We'll be going as soon as I get the gas pumped."

Sandy, relieved to have Terry as his protector, opened the car with a shaky hand and crawled inside. He felt smaller than his actual stature.

"We don't want trouble, mister. Didn't know he was your kid."

"Kid. You think he's my *kid*."

"Yeah. Thought he was just a fag walking around our town."

"Does he look like a spent cigarette butt to you? He looks like a full-grown man to me."

"A what?"

"You really need to learn the definitions of things. A

'fag' is a cigarette butt."

"No, it ain't. It's a queer."

"No, son. You're queer."

"Hey! I ain't no ass-muncher!"

"Queer means strange and unusual. You are queer; nobody treats strangers like you are. Nobody, that is, with any manners. Now, scoot on, youngsters, and go play with your…balls." Terry noticed they held a basketball. "It looks like you have somewhere to be. Leave us alone like good little boys and prove your parents had the good sense to teach you how to treat others."

The teenagers looked confused. They didn't know what kind of gay men they'd encountered but didn't want him confusing them more. "Come on. Let's go. Ain't nobody here worth our time."

"Good choice."

Terry finished pumping the gas and slowly climbed behind the steering wheel. "You okay, honey?"

"Yeah. My big, brave warrior."

Terry chuckled. "Let's get going."

They kept driving eastward, no destination in mind.

"Hey, Terry? Next chance we get, turn to the left, okay?"

"Left? North?"

"Uh huh. I think we can go through the mountains that way."

"You got it; north it is."

Five minutes later, a solid, paved, two-lane highway

became their next route. "Where are we?"

Sandy looked at the atlas. "Says we're nearly in Colorado."

"Colorado, huh? Pretty country, there."

"Maybe we can go skiing!"

"It's May, Sandy. I'm not sure there is any snow."

Sandy sat back in his seat and pouted. He crossed his arms over his slight chest and looked toward Terry. "That's not fair."

"Next time we take a road trip, we can do it in November, okay?"

Sandy's mood improved. "Okay. I'd like that."

They kept driving north, no particular idea what they would encounter.

"Do you want something to drink?" Sandy reached over the seat to grab the bag holding two more bottles of wine.

"We really shouldn't. I'm driving. You can have some, though. I won't mind."

"A little wouldn't hurt, would it? I don't want to drink alone." Another pout changed Terry's mind.

"Oh, alright. Just a little."

Thirty minutes later, the bottle drained, Terry and Sandy felt happier; the wine gave both some liquid courage.

"Maybe we could take a chance and drive the speed limit, now?"

Sandy shrugged. "I'm okay. Drive ten over if you want. Nobody's on the road but us, anyway."

Terry nodded. The mountainous highway had many blind spots and hairpin curves, but he felt like he could handle anything with Sandy at his side.

The sun fell quickly behind the high mountain peaks. The Rocky Mountains hid many secrets.

"It's getting dark. Wanna find a place to stop?"

"We brought the tent?"

"We did."

"Then, my dear mountain man, we can just find a clearing and pitch the tent. I'll keep an eye out."

"Nothing but sheer cliffs everywhere, Sandy. I don't know if we'll find a place soon."

"I think we'll be alright."

"The only lights outside come from the headlights. I'll have to slow down."

"Then, that's alright. We can slow down. I would rather reach the end of our journey alive than smashed against rocks or blown up in the car."

Terry shuddered. Still tipsy, he began to sober enough to realize the truth in Sandy's words.

"Look. What's that?"

Sandy looked in the direction Terry indicated. A small car-park lay right in front of them. "We can stop there, can't we? If we're careful, we can put the car in front of the tent, so it doesn't get hit by another driver."

Terry agreed and pulled into the small clearing. He looked up when something clicked downward onto the parking space. "Huh."

"What?"

"Rocks are falling."

"I'm sure it'll be fine, Terry. Let's just put the tent over…" Sandy looked around the parking area big enough for four cars. "…there."

Terry turned the Passat around, so the trunk faced the area Sandy indicated. "Okay. Just what we need, alright? That means, food and tent, only."

"Aww. No night clothes?"

"Naw. We're in the great outdoors. We'll sleep in the buff."

"I think I'll sleep in my clothes, if it's all the same to you."

Terry's head leaned back, and he roared with laughter. "That will be fine. I didn't think you'd go for that. We keep our clothes on."

"Deal."

They pitched the tent and put the cooler and cookie tin in the tent. "Wine?"

"Nah. Get that bag of water and Cokes. We should save the wine."

"Alright." Sandy took the food and drinks from the car and tucked them into the large, six-person tent.

They watched the sun disappear behind the mountain peaks in the west, sitting arm-in-arm. "It is so peaceful here. I could stay here forever!" Sandy didn't know how prophetic his simple statement would be.

Terry nodded and pulled Sandy closer to him and kissed the top of his head.

When they couldn't see their hands in front of their

faces, they retired into the tent. A small, electric lantern lit their environment and they enjoyed small talk, oatmeal cookies, and soda.

Sandy, in the middle of a sentence, yawned and stretched. "Oh my! Where did that come from?"

"It's been a long day, sweetness. We should tuck in and get some sleep."

Sandy agreed and unrolled the thin sleeping bags, laying one under them and the other to cover both.

"What's that noise?"

Terry tilted his head. "Sounds like more pebbles falling from above. Probably just some critters settling in for the night."

"Cr…critters?"

"Yeah. We are outside, Sandy."

Sandy nodded but felt apprehensive until he finally fell asleep. Terry waited until he heard Sandy's breath even off before he closed his own eyes.

Morning broke and the two awoke in each other's arms. Sandy tilted his head up and kissed Terry's chin. "Good morning, sleepyhead. Time to get on the road?"

Terry mumbled but sat and stretched. "I s'pose so."

They packed everything and rolled the sleeping bags before leaving the tent.

"Oh my god!" Sandy gasped; a huge boulder rested atop the Passat. The car totaled, neither knew what they would do.

"How did we sleep through that?" Terry turned to

look at the tent. Several large rocks, and small boulders had crushed the tent. "We got out right in time."

"I didn't hear those rocks hit the tent, baby." Sandy looked distressed when he peered through the opening. "Terry?"

"Mh hmm?"

"Look."

Terry, still staring at the boulders that had destroyed their sleeping and traveling arrangements took a moment to realize Sandy wanted him to look into the tent.

"Is that…"

"Feet, Terry. That's feet. *Our* feet! We're…we're…"

"Dead."

Sandy started to walk around in circles, stressed and distraught. "We're dead? How are we dead? We're right here!"

"I think we're ghosts, Sandy." Terry refused to put too much thought into their new situation. After all, they'd be in heaven or hell if such places existed. Instead, they stood together, alone on the side of the road, squashed beneath boulders in their corporeal bodies.

"Ghosts." Sandy began to cry. He sat hard on the boulder that had landed on his own head. "Dead. Ghosts. What are we to do, now, Terry?"

"I suppose whatever we want to, Sandy."

Sandy stopped sobbing and looked at Terry. He didn't see worry or distress. Instead, Terry looked bemused and a little happy.

"How can you be happy? We're dead!"

"What are we going to do about that, Sandy? Can we change it? No. So, we, er, live with our new situations. Think of it this way. We wanted an adventure; we've got one! What a grand adventure it will be to walk around unencumbered by bodies. We can haunt people, now. Won't that be fun?"

Sandy started to think about what Terry said. "We can't get drunk anymore. I guess, though, we can't die, either. We'll look like our beautiful selves forever."

"You did say you wanted to stay here forever. Maybe this is karma telling us it's okay to."

Sandy realized the logic in Terry's words. "Okay. We can try this. How long?"

"Forever."

***

Troy and Teresa, lounging against pillows on the bed, heard a news report on the television: *two men were crushed while camping on a roadside turn-around parking area in the Rocky Mountains just south of Boulder, Colorado. The images, we must warn you, are graphic.*

Teresa gasped. "Troy! Isn't that your dads' car?"

Troy, half-asleep, glanced toward the television. "Bright yellow Passat?"

"Yeah."

Troy immediately awoke. "That's Daddy T's car! Look at the plates! TST. That's their car!" He started shouting and screaming. He couldn't believe he'd lost the men who'd raised him to be a successful man against the odds of *normal* society.

Teresa grabbed Troy around the shoulders and let him cry into her shoulder. "I know, sweetheart. I know. They were good men. We will miss them so much."

"I have to go get them. They need to be brought back here."

"Brought back? I thought they said they wanted to be cremated. Can't that be done in Colorado?"

Troy sobbed into Teresa's chest, unable to formulate words.

She held him for several minutes before he'd cried himself dry. Still sobbing, though without tears, he pulled away. "We need to get my dads."

"I know, Troy. We'll go right away."

"I have to know where they are."

"Rockies, just south of Boulder. That's what the news reporter said. We can start by calling around police departments to see what town they were taken to."

Troy appreciated Teresa's sensible approach to the devastating news. "Can you help me with that?"

"You go shower. I'll make some calls."

Troy kissed Teresa and crawled weakly from the bed.

Teresa discovered the car was found on a county highway thirty-five miles south of Boulder, Colorado. They took the next flight to retrieve Terry and Sandy's bodies.

"Sheriff Brooks, I presume? I'm Troy Tatar. I'm here for my dads' bodies."

"Mr. Tatar, I'm afraid there's nothing we could have done. I'm sorry for your loss. Your 'dads', you say?"

"Yes. Is there a problem with that?"

Teresa felt tension tighten Troy's body and squeezed his hand.

"I didn't mean anything by that. I just didn't know. We don't get a lot of partnerships around here is all."

Troy felt his body slump and he dropped into a chair. "I'm sorry. This is just too much."

"I'm sure it is. If you would like to collect yourself, I can take you to your fathers."

Troy stood and, with Teresa's help, followed the sheriff.

"That's them?" Two drawers were pulled from the refrigerated cadaver storage compartment.

"It is. I know, it's not easy to identify them, I'm sorry. We have their wallets; this is merely a formality."

Troy was able to easily identify the bodies based on physique and clothing styles. "I can't see their faces, but those are their wedding rings and the clothes look right."

They agreed to speak with a local funeral home to cremate the men locally. That way, it'd be easier to transport them back to California."

"Honey, do you think you want to do them a favor? I mean, you love them so much, but what if they don't want to sit on our mantel forever?"

Troy shrugged. "What do you suggest?"

"They went off on this trip for some reason, didn't they?"

"Yeah, but they didn't talk to anyone. Their neighbors said they had no destination, just a road trip to parts unseen."

"There's your answer."

Teresa and Troy had a quiet ceremony for Terry and Sandy in a small chapel in Evergreen, Colorado. The minister let the two sit there while he spoke words of peace and enlightenment. Troy felt the entire event seemed farcical. After all, his dads did not follow religious prescripts. They may have been spiritual and attended a non-denominational church, but they did not follow any established faith.

"That's over." Troy sounded relieved more than peaceful. "We should get going."

"Alright. Are we flying back?"

"Thought I'd rent a car and drive home. I'm in no hurry."

"Alright, sweetheart. We can drive."

They got a rental car and started on their trek. The sheriff gave them a map and showed them where Terry and Sandy had been found.

"It's starting to get dark. Should we wait until tomorrow?"

"I don't think so. We should be alright. I just want to get back." Troy put the urns into a cardboard box on the back floorboard to keep them from tilting.

"Okay. Let's get going, then."

They drove south, following the route marked on the map from the sheriff.

"What's that?"

Three cars stopped on the side of the road. People stood outside and watched down the highway.

"They seem to be looking for something."

"They look like they're looking *at* something." Teresa leaned forward. "There's something there! Look! On the side of the road by that outcropping of boulders."

Troy slowed the car and pulled in beside the other cars. He sat, completely still, when he realized where they parked. "Oh my god!" He pulled the car back into the road.

"What are you doing?"

"Look at the place where I stopped. There's something on the ground. It's blood."

"Blood?"

"Yeah. That's my dads' last resting place."

Troy stepped from the car and looked at the other spectators. "What are you looking at?"

"They're there. Look!" Troy squinted and looked in the direction the teenage boy pointed. He could make out figures, nearly translucent. They looked like watery shadows. The two held what seemed to be hands and trudged down the road without a care in the world.

"Could that be..."

"I think so, Troy." Teresa stood beside Troy holding

the box containing the two urns. "We should put them to rest here, Troy."

"Whatcha got there? Is that *them*?"

"Them?"

"Yeah, the two poor guys who got crushed to death here."

Troy choked on his next words; he couldn't get them out. Tears streamed down his face.

"Oh shit! You ain't kidding, are you? That's them? I wanna say something for 'em."

"You do?" Troy looked, disbelieving, at the young man.

"I do. Lost my gran and grandpa up here a few years back. Didn't get to say nothing for them. Could I? What were their names?"

Teresa smiled sweetly at the boy. "That would be very nice. Their names were Terry and Sandy."

The boy nodded and looked forward to the shadows continuing down the road. "That's Terry and Sandy. They were good men. They took good care of that what was theirs. They loved well and they are still loved. I wish them happiness in their forever."

He bowed his head and said a prayer before opening his eyes. "We should put those ashes here, too. They'd like that."

Troy looked at the box holding the urns. "I think they would. Would you help me?"

The boy took the pinkish urn and carefully tugged the lid.

"All or some?"

"All." Troy did the same with the larger, brass urn.

"Where you want it?"

"I think away from where they died. Maybe over the edge? They could fly with the wind."

"That's a wonderful idea, Troy."

Everyone stood back and watched the ceremony unfold; Terry and Sandy flew into the breeze, unnaturally swirling together as though in a final embrace.

Everyone present stood silently for over fifteen minutes, watching the dance of ash until it finally dissipated into the sky and against the cliffs below.

"I guess they're happy."

Everyone turned to leave. Out of the corner of his eye, Troy thought he saw his fathers wave their final good-bye.

Terry and Sandy walked along the quiet mountain highway, holding hands and enjoying their forever future.

Saxon Bryce

Finnegan's Wake

Tim Finnegan walked around, hod on his shoulder. Sometimes he'd have it filled with bricks, other times, it'd be full of mortar to set the brick. He knew he'd need to make plenty of money to raise himself and his family to a higher standard of living.

To get himself through his torturous and hard-working days, he'd been known to take a drink or two of cheap whisky. Sadly, having a drink became a part of Tim's life from infancy; born with the love of liquor.

One morning, on his way to work, Tim stopped by a local pub; cheerful music poured onto the street when he opened the door. He knew he had work to do but hadn't eaten breakfast and needed something in his stomach. Whisky, his choice of drink, became his breakfast that morning.

"Timmy, mate. You have to get on to work, don't you? Have to pay for the rent next week. You drink most of your pay away. Get on, then. Go on and go to work."

Tim grumbled and pointed at the rocks glass in front of him and put two fingers into the air. "I'll get to work as soon as I've broken my fast, if it is all the same to you."

The bartender shook his head and looked Tim in the eye. He looked sober, so he poured two-fingers into the glass. "Your funeral, mate."

Two hours later, Tim stood from the stool and stumbled to the door. When it opened, he growled and covered his face with his arm. "Who turned the spotlights on?"

"That's just the sun, Tim. You been inside too long. Give 'er a few. You'll get used to it. Off, now. Go on. Get to work. The missus won't be thanking me for keeping you so long.

Tim waved his arm abruptly behind his back. He didn't need a lecture from some young man behind a bar. "I can hold my liquor, young buck. Keep your opinions to yourself."

The bartender ignored Tim. He'd heard it often enough to know Tim would be back later in the day or tomorrow morning at the latest.

"What's wrong with Timmy-boy this morning?"

The bartender shrugged. "Don't know, do I? He said he needed breakfast."

The rest of the bar patrons nodded. They all knew Tim Finnegan well enough.

***

Tim stumbled down the road. Thankfully, his current worksite wasn't far from the pub. He knew the police would arrest him if he drove drunk.

"Timmy, where have you been? We've been waiting on you. Get yourself up there and start packing mortar around those bricks. You know you were supposed to be here bright at eight."

"I know, I know. I can't help that I got delayed on the way."

The foreman stood at the side, his hands on his waist. He looked deeply into Tim's bloodshot eyes and shook his head. "Don't go dying on me today, Tim. We have too much work to do." He didn't address the heavy scent of alcohol oozing through Tim's pores or that his best brick-layer came in drunk nearly every day.

Tim shrugged. He felt confident he'd walked enough of the whisky off to be useful. He filled his hod with mortar and climbed the short ladder. "Can't fall too far from here." He took care of his business and worked until the sun fell too far below the horizon to offer useful light.

Thirsty, he dropped the hod and dragged it to Paddy's pub. He knew they'd quench his thirst. "Finnegan! You lived through the day, did ya?" Paddy joked. Tim got a good laugh out of it.

"Aye. Time for a refresher."

Tim spent several hours at Paddy's. He sang all the old standards he'd learned since finding his favorite hangout. Finally, Paddy turned the lights on.

"Last call's been over for half an hour, mates. Time to shuffle your arses back to your wives."

Everyone looked toward Tim. He sat, head bowed, shoulders slumped. "He sleeping?"

"Nah. He's alright, ain't you, Timmy-boy?"

"Yeah. Fine. Just fine. Lead me home, would you, fellas?"

Two of his best mates took him by the elbows and helped him off the bar stool and toward the door. "We'll get you home, Tim. Come on. We're going to drive you."

"I can't drive. Too drunk. The cops'll take me in."

"No, you don't understand. We will take you home. I'm driving."

Tim leaned back to focus on the man to his left. "You sure? I've been drinking a lot. Not suited to driving."

"Yeah, I'm sure, Tim. I'll be alright driving while you're drunk."

The men chuckled. This wasn't the first time they'd left Tim Finnegan's car at Paddy's Pub. Paddy would drive it around to the back and leave it locked up until Tim could collect it.

***

The next morning, like each previous one, he stopped by Paddy's, though he didn't feel quite himself.

"What's happened to you, Tim? You look like death took you for a spin and spit you out wet and miserable."

"I don't feel quite myself today, Paddy. Perhaps just a wee dram this morning."

"Wee dram? You have been having a rough day, haven't you? I haven't seen you ask for such a small drink in seventeen years or more."

Tim shrugged. He knew he could out drink most anyone; he just didn't quite feel right today.

"That's all for now. Perhaps, after I have my first, I'll feel more like myself."

Paddy agreed and poured a little more than a shot of whisky into a glass for his best patron. He left the man to his drink and began wiping imaginary dust from the bar top.

"Another round, my good man." Tim sounded more himself and took three more glasses, three-fingers each, before grabbing his hod, reached for it five times before he found the real one and not the mirror images.

"Time to go to work. Place ain't buildin' itself."

"Careful, Tim. Want to see you this evening, alive and all in one piece."

Tim waved behind him and stumbled to work.

"Tim, you gotta stop this drinking."

"What drinking? I'm perfectly fine." Tim hiccupped his response to his boss.

"You damn well better be, boy! I ain't got good enough insurance to keep paying for a lay about who drinks all day."

"Lay about? I do my job. You know I do."

"Aye, you do that. I guess I need to lay off. Don't want my best mason all upset and quitting on me."

"No, you don't."

Tim climbed the ladder; two rungs higher this time.

He noticed the house began to look like a house rather than a wooden skeleton with a few glass windows and brick skin. "You're doin' a fine job, Timmy-boy. A fine job, indeed."

Today felt hotter than the previous days. Summer came closer with each passing hour. The heat beat down on the workers. Tim felt especially exposed to the fiery heat. He began to feel dizzy and he started shaking. The alcohol still heavy in his system didn't help him this day.

He fell, refusing numerous offers of water to quench his thirst and cool his skin. "No time for lifeless water."

"Tim!"

Tim's body tumbled ten feet downward to the ground. His body spun and he hit, head-first, on the concrete pad poured for a car park.

Blood oozed from his damaged skull. When the men arrived, they could clearly see his skull cracked open, though, thankfully, his brains were not exposed.

"C'mon! Let's get him out of that dirt. Who's got a truck we can put him in the back and take him to the hospital."

Several hours passed, and the doctor came from the back where Tim had been taken when they arrived.

"I'm afraid to tell you that I can do nothing more for your friend. He's lost a lot of blood; he may live, he may not. He's alive, right now, though he's unconscious. Do you want to let him stay here for observations or take him somewhere?"

"His wife'll want to see him. We'll take him there. She'll take care of him until he's better. You have him all cleaned up?"

"As well as we could, yes."

His coworkers helped Tim from a wheelchair into the front seat of his conveyance to the hospital. "Hang in there, Timmy. You'll be home soon enough."

Tim, barely conscious due to heavy pain killers, alcohol still running through his bloodstream, and the injury to his head, slumped forward in the seat.

"Jesus Christ! Watch his noggin! He busted it right open, remember? Not like that big white bandage didn't give it away!"

Sheepish, the man who let him fall forward tugged him into the seat and buckled the seatbelt around his torso and hips. "Should be alright, now."

Everyone followed the truck to Finnegan's house. Tim, not a small man, would need all their help into the house.

"Think his bedroom's on the top floor?"

"Hope not. Can't carry him that far, can we?"

"We better."

"Just hope his wife doesn't bust our skulls for letting him do that to himself."

"That's the truth."

"Why didn't anyone stop him from climbing that ladder? Didn't the boss see he was drunk?"

"Don't know. Guess he'd have to have known, huh? Suppose the job paid enough for him to turn his head.

Timmy's the best, you know?"

"Aye. That, he is."

Mrs. Finnegan stared out the front door when six pickup trucks rolled to a stop. She twisted her apron in her hands, worried they would tell her the worst. When four men walked to the front truck and opened the passenger door, she wailed and ran forward. Two more men caught her on the way to Tim's limp body.

His legs tripped over grass and cracks on the sidewalk and his head lolled oddly to the side though he had a huge grin on his face.

"Maggie, my love, do help by opening the door?"

Maggie Finnegan turned and reluctantly rushed to the house. She kept turning back to the others, fretting and worrying.

"What'd he do? Did he get in a fight? What's that on his head for?"

"He fell off a ladder, Mrs. Finnegan. We took him to the doctor. He said he could be alright, but he lost a lot of blood. Said we could bring him home. We thought you'd want to be the one to care for 'im."

She nodded, agreeing that she did want to care for her injured husband. "Aye. Thank you for thinking to bring him home. Can't right afford him to be out of work, you know?"

"Not working, are you, Mrs. Finnegan?" She shook her head. "We'll pitch in and help around here until Timmy's back on his feet."

"That would be appreciated; thank you."

They were lucky, Tim and Maggie's bedroom was on the first floor. They only had to clear four steps to the front porch.

"Here you go, Timmy. Get yourself in there."

Maggie Finnegan turned down the covers and helped the men pull his boots and jeans off. "I suppose he can stay in his shirt for now. I'll clean him up later."

The men left the bedroom and allowed Maggie to do her best with her husband. They quietly walked through the front door and to their trucks after making plans to return in two-days' time to help around the house.

****

Morning came and Maggie stood to make breakfast and coffee for Tim before she remembered he probably shouldn't eat very much. Instead of eggs, sausage, beans, and biscuits, she made oatmeal and tea.

"Tim, you doddering old fool. I've made you something to eat. You should try to put something in your gullet so you can get better quick and back to work. Need your money, you know." Maggie set a tray on the night table and tried to lift Tim, but he was much too heavy.

"Leave me be, Maggie. My head feels like a ton of bricks fell on it. What happened, anyway?"

"You fell on a ton of bricks you old drunk. If you didn't start your day at the pub, you'd not have fallen off that ladder and broke your head."

"I did? Well, ain't that something. I've been working like this for over twenty-five years and God finally reminded me that wasn't a good idea." He leaned back and tried to rest the back of his head in his palms but winced in pain, pulling back a reddened hand. "S'pose I'm bleeding. Got more wraps for it?"

Tim Finnegan seemed less concerned over his own injury than his wife did, though it was his head split wide open.

"Eat. You have to eat. You haven't got enough blood to redden your cheeks when you speak such nonsense, Tim. You need to eat."

"Eat, eat, eat. Woman! Leave me be!"

And with that, Maggie left the bedroom, slamming the door hard and loud. Tim shouted in pain from the noise and from the gust of wind that seemed to vibrate past his head. "Guess I deserve this headache."

He ate two bites of oatmeal and tried a sip of tea before he grabbed his stomach and bent over. The food settled on his empty stomach and caused him to retch.

"I should probably stop drinking."

Maggie stood outside the bedroom door, still worried about her husband. She seemed to feel his pain and discomfort.

Tim slept better the second night after taking three pain pills prescribed by the doctor. A few times during the night, he'd wake up and take a swallow of the bottle of whisky hidden at the back of the nightstand.

Maggie entered the bedroom the next morning

carrying a tray of toast and more tea. There were pats of butter and jam on the side if he felt he could keep that down.

"Tim. Maybe you can eat some toast instead of oat…" The tray slammed to the ground. Tim lay in an unnatural position, his eyes half-open, his mouth gaping. Maggie stepped forward tentatively and put her hand over his face. She felt no breath.

She screamed and ran from the house just as the men from Tim's work pulled up. She sat on the porch steps, clutching her waist and crying into her knees.

"Mrs. Finnegan. What has happened? Is Tim alright?"

"Tim's dead. He's dead, I say."

"Dead? I thought he was on the mend?"

"Aye, me too. He tried to eat yesterday morn' without luck but kept some chicken broth down last night. He seemed sleeping restful but this morning…" she waved at the house. "Just go see for yourself. He's in the bed."

Two men entered the house while the others stayed with Maggie. They returned shortly after, sad and at a loss. "Mrs. Finnegan, I'm so sorry."

Maggie returned to the bedroom to clean up her husband. The men did work around the house and offered to help her wash Tim and roll him into a sheet for display.

They discussed having a wake. "Tim was quite the popular bloke, you know?"

Maggie nodded. "Aye. He was, at that. A wake would give his friends some time to say goodbye."

The plans settled; the men took off to announce a wake for that evening. Maggie didn't want a corpse in her house for too long.

The door was blocked open, so nobody needed to knock to enter. Various spirits, food, and memories rested on tables and trays around Tim's body. He held the post of honor in the center of the living room.

A woman from the pub stepped to Tim's body and began to wail as though she had lost her husband. "He's so clean. Have you ever seen such a clean corpse? Tim, my dear friend, why did you have to die?"

"Shut your mouth, Biddie O'Brien!" Paddy McGee stood on the other side of Tim's corpse and glanced at Maggie who looked suspiciously upon Biddie.

"I'm sure you're quite wrong, Biddie," Maggie O'Connor, another guest and friend of Tim's said, trying to keep the angst going. Well, her words weren't welcome and Biddie, before Maggie realized it, punched the other woman in the mouth; Maggie fell backwards, sprawled unladylike across the floor.

Before anyone could stop anything, the woman began a row in the middle of the floor that escalated to include every person in the living room.

Men punched men, women tore at women's clothing and hair. The melee was quite involved, and everyone was either atop or below everyone else.

Mickey Maloney stood to the side and tilted his head

just in time for a flying bucket of whisky to cruise past his head and fell onto the bed where Tim lie dormant and lifeless.

The barrel broke and the whisky splattered everywhere, all over Tim. Heaven must not have been ready for Tim, however. The man sat up, licked his lips and looked around the room.

He tugged at the sheet around him and noticed he wore no clothes beneath. After a few minutes, he realized what was happening.

"Why are you whirling the whisky around like that? Thundering Jesus, do you think I'm dead?"

Maggie Finnegan screamed and fainted dead away.

From the Diaphragm

Saxon Bryce

About the Author

What can I say? I love music and I equally love prose. I once watched a movie based on a song and thought it interesting. Then, I read a short story based on a song and thought, "I would like to do that!"

With that, *From the Diaphragm* was imagined. It has been a long trek, taking nearly a year from concept to completion of this little book of short stories.

Why short stories? A coworker of mine suggested short stories. That was a decade ago! I know, I'm a slow-starter. I like to think of this as a bathroom reader.

What about me? Well, I'm a concept, too. I'm just a writer who loves music. I try to sing, I try to write, and I try to keep the peace. I like calm; it is very conducive to productivity. Don't you think so?

My name is unique and boy, did I get teased for it! I mean, my first name is a last name, and my last name is a first name. My mom and dad were quite the jokers, I tell you! I survived my childhood by doing well in school and keeping my head down. That is my advice to anyone with such creative parents. My education did not suffer for my name. Many teachers found it refreshing that, even though unique, my name is easy to pronounce.

I'm neither here, nor there. I'm not overly important, nor am I insignificant. I feel that I'm equal to all members of the world. I merely hope you may find it in your heads and hearts to enjoy my short tales and perhaps leave a friendly review.

Thank you, in advance!

Saxon Bryce

From the Diaphragm

Credits

Title	Performed by:	Writer
The Gypsy Rover	Elton Hayes	Leo Maguire
Harden my Heart	Quarterflash	Marv Ross
Willie McBride	Liam Clancy	Eric Bogle
Careless Whisper	Wham	George Michael & Andrew Ridgeley
Home from the Sea	Liam Clancy	Tony Banks
Fiddler's Green	The Irish Rovers	John Conolly
Maid of Culmore	Celtic Thunder	Unknown
Big, Bad John	Jimmy Dean	Jimmy Dean & Roy Acuff
Sweet Molly Malone	The Dubliners	James Yorkston
The Way	Fastball	Tony Scalzo
Finnegan's Wake	The Dubliners	Unknown